W9-AJQ-716
3 4028 09113 2713
HARRIS COUNTY PUBLIC LIBRARY

THE IT GIRL

KATY BIRCHALL

ALADDIN
New York London Toronto Sydney New Delhi

This book is a work of fiction. Any references to historical events, real people, or real places are used fictitiously. Other names, characters, places, and events are products of the author's imagination, and any resemblance to actual events or places or persons, living or dead, is entirely coincidental.

ALADDIN
An imprint of Simon & Schuster Children's Publishing Division
1230 Avenue of the Americas, New York, New York 10020
First Aladdin hardcover edition June 2016
First published in Great Britain in 2015 by Egmont UK Limited

Designed by Laura Lyn DiSiena
The text of this book was set in Electra.
Manufactured in the United States of America 0516 FFG
2 4 6 8 10 9 7 5 3 1
This title has been cataloged with the Library of Congress.
ISBN 978-1-4814-6362-1 (hc)
ISBN 978-1-4814-6363-8 (eBook)

For Mum, Dad, Robert, and Charles

I SET JOSIE GRAHAM ON FIRE.

And, okay, yes it was bad, but it was an accident and not *entirely* my fault. Everyone thinks I did it on purpose. They think Mrs. Ginnwell is a hero.

If you ask me, Mrs. Ginnwell made the whole thing worse. A little bit of water would have sorted everything out just fine. It was only the ends of her hair, and a fire extinguisher was a very dramatic plan of action. I mean, Josie was already having a pretty bad day considering I'd just set her on fire and everything, and the next thing she knew she was covered head to toe in that white foamy stuff that always looks like it might be fun to play in but probably isn't. (I think Josie looked more in shock—and a little bit itchy—than like she was having fun.)

I was kind of in shock myself. I'd never set fire to anyone before so the whole incident came as a bit of a surprise. The closest I've been to any kind of arson was when I was little and I put my dad's wallet on the fire log to see what would happen. I mean, who leaves their wallet lying around in the same room as a toddler? Not my father anymore that's for sure. But I still think he looks at me a little bit suspiciously on cold nights.

Oh, and there *was* that time I almost burned down Dad's study. But those two times are IT.

And you know what? This is partly Josie Graham's fault too. Because really, she should not have been (a) leaning on her hand so close to a Bunsen burner and (b) wearing so much hairspray to school.

I'm just jealous because I don't have the time, let alone the skills, for hairspray. Once Dad has eventually wrestled the duvet cover away from me, I have about ten minutes tops to get ready.

My dad would never buy me hairspray anyway. He's so old-fashioned, especially when it comes to his twelve-year-old daughter. I remember one time in a drugstore I asked him if he would buy me eyeliner. He burst out laughing and made me go fetch some Theraflu. I think this is VERY hypocritical as some of the women my dad has dated have worn a LOT of dark eyeliner. How would he feel if, when he introduced them, I laughed in their face and gave them a mug of hot lemon acetaminophen instead?

Hmm . . . I might consider this for the really annoying ones that get brought home.

A wobbling Mrs. Ginnwell definitely wasn't laughing as she marched me into Ms. Duke's office mumbling something incoherent about fire in the classroom and pyromaniac tendencies.

"Sorry, Mrs. Ginnwell, I didn't quite understand that. What did you say?" Ms. Duke asked, rising from her desk with a look of concern.

Ms. Duke really suits her office. Which sounds strange when I say it out loud, but it just goes with her overall vibe. She's new to the school too. We were both new in September, although obviously she's a bit more senior being principal and everything. I just started seventh grade. Everything considered, I think she has managed to set the better impression out of the two of us so far. This is not great seeing as she gives out detentions and makes people pick up trash from behind the bike rack.

So even though she's only been in that office for a semester and I'm not entirely sure what it looked like before she arrived, it matches her. For example, it's all very neat. Ms. Duke is very formal and smartly dressed. She looks more like those businesswomen who are always on their hands-free cell phones in train stations barking things like, "That's just not good enough, Jeffrey," than a principal at a co-ed school.

I like the way she can pull off a pantsuit though. I think if ever I was going to work in an office I would like to wear a pantsuit and look authoritative like Ms. Duke does. And her dark hair is always so neatly pinned and her makeup never smudged. She is very intimidating.

Even more so when you've just set your classmate's hair on fire.

"Chemistry class . . . Anna . . . Anna set . . . hair . . . Josie Graham on fire!" Mrs. Ginnwell finally spluttered.

Mrs. Ginnwell is neither authoritative nor intimidating. She kind of reminds me of a parrot. But not a cool one that would chill with a pirate. An overzealous one that swoops around your head, squawking and whacking you unexpectedly in the face with its wings.

"Is Josie all right?" Ms. Duke asked in alarm.

Mrs. Ginnwell nodded, her curled strawberry-blond hair frizzing around her sweaty forehead. "Fine. Although her hair is quite singed and covered in foam."

"I see," Ms. Duke replied, and I swear I saw her smirk for

a second. If she did, it was gone in an instant when she caught my eye. "And no one else was hurt in this incident?"

"No." Mrs. Ginnwell shook her head.

"Well in that case, Anna, you can have a seat and, Jenny, why don't you pop into the teachers' lounge and ask someone to cover your lesson for a bit while you get a cup of coffee."

Mrs. Ginnwell nodded and slowly released her grip on me. She gave me a very pointed look, as if when let loose I would pull out a flamethrower from my locker and burn the school to the ground. Which is a completely ridiculous thought for her to entertain because last semester I did an excellent essay on penguins. No one who puts that much effort and emotional maturity into a seventh-grade essay about penguins would be spending their free time plotting to destroy their school.

I sat down slowly into the leather chair opposite Ms. Duke, who was settling into her chair behind the desk. The heavy wooden door closed loudly as Mrs. Ginnwell escaped, still glaring at me, and there was a moment of silence as Ms. Duke straightened the forms she had been filling in before we interrupted her afternoon.

"So, why don't you explain to me exactly what happened?"

I took a deep breath and told her how we had been in our chemistry class and Josie and I had been partnered together, which, by the way, neither of us were too happy about. I didn't tell Ms. Duke that part though.

I assumed she would know that it had been an unhappy arrangement. Josie is one of the most popular girls in our grade. She's best friends with Queen Bee, Sophie Parker, and they're always hanging out with the popular boys like Brendan Dakers and James Tyndale. Josie spends her weekends partying and comes to school wearing a full face of makeup and her hair sprayed perfectly into place.

I spend my weekends reading comics, watching *CSI* with my dad, and complaining about my life to my yellow Labrador, called Dog, who is the only creature on this planet who listens to me. And I can only get him to listen if I'm holding a bit of bacon.

So I skipped out the part of the story where Josie looked miserably at Brendan, who she was clearly hoping to be partnered with, and then came to sit next to me with a big sigh and no greeting. She didn't even look at me when I went, "Howdy, partner," in a courageous attempt to lighten the atmosphere.

I really don't know why that was the greeting I went with.

She couldn't be bothered to do the experiment, so I just got on with it. Now, technically, Mrs. Ginnwell had not explained the Bunsen burner part of the experiment yet as everyone was putting on their lab coats and goggles. But some people were taking their time, and Josie, leaning on her hand, kept glancing at Brendan, laughing at whatever he was saying to her and flicking her hair dramatically.

I guess this is where it kind of becomes my fault. I should have waited until we were told to start up the Bunsen burners, but I went ahead and turned ours on.

There are a few very important things to remember here:

1. I did not realize it was on the highest flame setting.
2. I did not realize that, just as I turned it on, Josie would flick her hairspray-laden locks in the direction that she did.
3. I did not realize that her hair was quite so flammable.
4. I did not realize that she would run around screaming rather than stay still so that throwing water at her became increasingly difficult, and my aim isn't that good anyway so I actually ended up just soaking myself.
5. I did not expect Mrs. Ginnwell to use so much foam that Josie resembled a poodle.

6. It should also be remembered that I have never been in any real trouble at school before this incident.
7. Apart from that time when I was six and Ben Metton ate my Doritos, so I locked him in the supply closet.
8. The whole fire incident is in fact very upsetting for me too as I didn't mean to do it, I feel awful, and now no one will want to stay friends with me, just like at my last school.

At this point I started crying.

Ms. Duke, who had been staring at me in shock, passed me a tissue. "Well, it sounds to me like it was an accident—" she began.

"Of course it was an accident!" I wailed, interrupting her. "I would never do that on purpose!"

There was a knock on the door, and I turned in my seat to see the school nurse slowly pop her head in. Ms. Duke beckoned her in, and she came forward happily. "I wanted to let you know, Ms. Duke, and you, Anna, that Josie is perfectly fine. Her hair is singed at the end and she'll have to have a haircut, but apart from that she is right as rain."

"She must hate me," I said glumly, staring at the damp, crumpled tissue in my hand.

"I'm sure she doesn't. She'll get over it," the nurse said jovially. "Her hair was so long and straggly anyway, a cut will probably improve things."

"Um, *thank* you, Tricia," Ms. Duke said pointedly. The nurse gave a cheerful shrug and left.

"There you go, that's something," Ms. Duke announced. "It was clearly an accident but one that could have had nasty consequences. We've been lucky, Anna."

I nodded gravely.

"I hope that from now on you won't begin any kind of experiment without instruction."

"I'm never going to do another experiment again."

"I hope you will. Chemistry is a fascinating subject, and I imagine you've learned an important lesson with regards to safety." She looked at me sternly. "Right, well, while we've established this wasn't intentional, I'm going to have to give you detention lasting the remainder of this semester so that you can reflect on the importance of caution. It starts tomorrow. And since it is the end of the day in about ten minutes, you can return to your classroom, gather your things, and go home."

"I'd rather not go back, to be honest."

"You don't need anything?"

"It's just my pencil case and books. People have probably thrown them in the trash by now."

"I'm sure that's not true." Ms. Duke gave a thin smile. "They all know it was an accident and no harm done. By tomorrow they'll have forgotten the whole thing."

It's worrying how clueless adults are sometimes.

WHEN MY DAD GETS CONCERNED, HIS EYEBROWS become very distracting.

I mean, he was *really concerned* about the situation. He made me sit down and everything. Dad and I rarely have conversations where we sit each other down. We both become very awkward.

The only other times that he's had to "sit me down to talk" about something were when I signed him up on a dating website because I didn't like his girlfriend at the time and he got all these suspicious e-mails that made her cry, and when I threw a pie at his head because he gave my Marvel comic book encyclopedia to a used bookshop and I happened to be holding a pie when he told me.

Dog later ate the pie, which had been cleaned up and put on a plate, because neither Dad nor I were keeping an eye on him during our "sitting down and talking" moment. This just made the whole situation worse because (a) Dad had apparently been looking forward to eating that pie and (b) Dog decided to rub his pie victory in Dad's face by vomiting it back up over Dad's sneakers.

I don't know why Dad was so angry. The only reason he owns sneakers is so that he can leave them by the door in the hope that women might think he works out.

Anyway, both those times that he "sat me down" his eyebrows were uncontrollable, and I knew, as soon as he asked me to sit to discuss the fire incident and his eyebrows immediately sprung into irrepressible motion, that he was having one of those moments when he wonders whether there is actually something genuinely wrong with me.

Like I don't question that every single day.

And honestly, I really was trying to concentrate on what he was saying, but his eyebrows were jumping around all over the place. It really is fascinating how they have such agility.

Sadly, he has not passed this impressive talent down to me.

"Are you even listening?"

"Of course!" I lied, unlocking my facial muscles from their state of concentration on this intricate eyebrow dance. I patted Dog absentmindedly as he lay next to me, clearly hoping for a treat after this act of loyalty in the face of a Dad Inquisition.

Dad's eyebrows furrowed. "Anastasia," he prompted, leaning forward and clasping his hands together in what I guessed was an attempt at giving an air of understanding.

"Nicholas." Two of us could play the I'm So Serious I'm Going to Use Your Full Name game.

Dad took a deep breath.

"I appreciate that changing schools is an upheaval, especially for a pre-teenager. I'm not mad at you—I know it was an accident. But if there's anything you want to, I don't know, *discuss*?"

"Like what?"

"I don't know. Pre-teenage things?"

Oh lord. I bet he wanted *feelings*. This was ambitious. I wasn't going to talk about that with my *dad*. It was embarrassing enough telling my two new and only friends, Jess and Danny, about each of the latest ways I had managed to humiliate myself and, by association, them too. I'd be lucky if I managed to hold on to those two for much longer the way things were going. Either way, there definitely wasn't any sharing happening with my dad.

"What pre-teenage things?"

"I don't know!" His eyebrows leaped frenziedly toward the ceiling. "Learning to be responsible?"

"Don't bother. I wouldn't listen anyway."

He narrowed his eyes. "Are you taking this seriously?"

"Yes I am taking this seriously. I set someone's hair on fire; it was dangerous and embarrassing. I will not be touching a Bunsen burner ever again without supervision. The whole school is going to hate me. I'm going to be a bigger loser than I was before. I hate my life."

"Well that's what I mean," he said gently. Seriously, I do one tiny thing like set someone on fire, and suddenly my dad feels the need to subject me to weird parental counseling. "It's just . . . at the last school . . . you weren't . . ." He trailed off.

"Ms. Popular?"

"That's not what I was going to say," Dad said, slumping back into the armchair where he usually sits on a Sunday afternoon with his Irish whiskey. "You weren't . . . settled. I just want to make sure that you're more confident with this new place."

I had to start a new school when we moved to London last year after Dad became a lot more in demand as a freelance journalist, and he needed to be where everything was happening. Weirdly, this happened after he wrote a really boring book about tanks used in the war or something that actually sold quite well. The book is dedicated to me, but I've never read it, which really bugs him. If you ask me, I should be the insulted one—yeah, Dad, it's every girl's dream to have a book about TANKS dedicated to them.

Incredibly, somehow the serious tank book led to serious articles on famous people—and they all seem to live in London or come here a lot. But it means he is at home a lot more than he used to be, which is good, although he does sometimes go to a celebrity party or whatever. Celebrities like Dad now because he writes big glossy features about them in trendy magazines rather than reporting on their sweat patches in a tiny column of a tabloid.

I think he felt pretty guilty about making me move, but I didn't mind. I didn't really have any friends at my old school, and even though I was a bit nervous about Dog settling down in London at first, he quickly made friends with a Pomeranian called Hamish down the road.

"Thanks, Dad. I appreciate your concern. But really? You can stop worrying."

He sighed, it being clear that I wasn't going to divulge any of the pre-teenage angst he was looking for. "Fine. Well, be more careful in future chemistry classes?"

"If they let me enter a science lab again in my lifetime, yes I'll be more careful. No Bunsen burners."

"I'm not going to ground you. It's not like you ever really go out anyway."

"Great, good chat, Dad, thanks."

He gave a last concerned eyebrow rise and then finally pulled himself up from his chair and left the room. I relaxed, and traitorous Dog immediately followed him just in case he was going in the direction of the kitchen.

Sadly for Dog, Dad went to his bedroom to get ready for his big date. Recently Dad has been seeing someone new who he still hasn't introduced me to. Not that I'm insulted.

Usually he's never with them long enough for me to meet them. I just pick up the phone every now and then and hear a different woman go, "Oh hi, sweetheart, is Nick there please?" and he makes a wild "say I'm not at home" gesture in the background as I explain that he's actually gone to Slovenia to find himself. I like to mix it up and throw in some pretty inspired reasons for his disappearance, such as he's modeling his new line of swimming trunks in Beirut, or he's in Peru training to be a spiritual guide.

This can be risky, however, because if Dad overhears, he throws things at me.

He's been seeing this girlfriend for a few months now though. He's really been quite disgusting about the whole thing. Combing his hair, wearing aftershave, and dancing—*dancing*—as he goes around the house. Honestly, I had to call Mom and tell her how embarrassed I was.

She was in India at the time so it was a bit crackly, but I think I managed to convey my disgust. Mom is a travel journalist, which means she's away a lot, but I don't mind. Sometimes she takes me with her to these amazing places, and then when she's in England and hasn't seen me in a while, she comes to stay with us too.

Mom and Dad were never married—or even together for very long. They met when they were both junior reporters, and in Dad's words "Rebecca was totally in love" with him, and in Mom's words she was "either very drunk, honey, or suffering from some kind of tropical disease that causes hallucinations." Either way, I was the outcome, and luckily they're really good friends, which makes things a lot easier.

When I was younger, I kept hoping they would get back together, like in *The Parent Trap* or whatever, but now I see that it's actually a lot better this way. Mom says they could never be together because Dad is too opinionated and the way he sneezes creeps her out. Dad says they could never be together because Mom never does the dishes and once mocked John Wayne's hat. I think it's actually because they're best friends, but hey, you've got to let adults believe what they want to believe.

"It sounds like he's in love, darling." Mom laughed down the phone as I explained Dad's recent antics. "Be nice to him." I'm not sure what other advice she gave me because as she spoke there was a lot of background noise at her end, and I think I could hear someone trying to sell cabbages for twenty rupees a pound. India seems like a very noisy place.

As Dad rummaged around in his bedroom, he decided to start lecturing me from upstairs. "I don't want any problems this evening. You're to stay home and behave," he instructed.

I found this comment unjustified considering I am very well behaved the majority of the time. I am hardly a trouble-maker and I don't get invited to any parties, so I don't really know what he was getting so anxious about.

The most recent time that I guess I wasn't the model of good behavior was when he had a housewarming party for our new place in London and all these people invaded, sauntering in with their wafts of expensive perfume and bottles of Chardonnay. I had to take their coats and walk around for the evening with trays of nibbles, listening to them tell Dad how adorable I was as they ignored me and picked up mini bruschettas from the tray.

Anyway there was this actor there who I overheard saying that he couldn't understand why Nick had that *dog* over there that looked like he would slobber all over the place and probably, by the look of the boy, wasn't even a good pedigree. I accidentally let Dog chew his hat.

Dad didn't make me sit down that time and have a talk about respecting my elders or anything, but he talked to me for about five billion hours the next day on the difference between fighter aircrafts and bomber aircrafts in the war.

I'm not sure if that was intended to be a punishment, but it sure felt like one.

"I'm just going to sit and watch movies with Dog. Have a little trust, Father."

"Not vampire movies?" He snorted with laughter at his own "joke."

This is not only unfunny but also grossly unfair considering he was the one who last week recommended the stupid people-slaying child-vampire movie to his twelve-year-old daughter, alone in the house with only a Labrador for company.

It's not as if Dog could protect me. He's afraid of spoons for crying out loud. Whenever we get out the big wooden salad spoon, he goes around in circles manically and barks his head off in fear. What would he do if a vampire strolled into the building? I'd had to disturb Dad on his date and make him come home and check to make sure there were no vampires around.

"When do I get to meet this girlfriend of yours?" I asked, ignoring the vampire movie comment and trying to change the subject.

"Soon enough," he said breezily, coming back into the room. "She's dying to meet you."

"I bet."

Dad did a last mirror-check in the hall. "Not bad for an old man, eh? I reckon I could pass for early thirties."

"Don't get ahead of yourself, Gramps. Anyone who talks about Eric Clapton with as much passion as you do could never be a day under forty."

"That's enough from you." He stood over me. "Are you going to be all right? No fires, yes?"

"No fires. No vampires."

"Call me if you need me." He gave my hair a ruffle, and then he shot me a long, hard look as though he was trying to read my face.

"Anna . . ." He hesitated. "You do . . . you do *like* it here in London, don't you?"

"Yes?"

"And you . . . well . . . never mind. Have a nice evening. Bye, Dog."

As the door closed, I got a very distinct feeling that my father wasn't telling me something.

From: jess.delby@zingmail.co.uk

To: anna_huntley@zingmail.co.uk

Subject: Are you a pyromaniac?!

So I tried looking for you after school but someone said you'd gone home early. And I've been trying to call and you're not picking up your home phone or cell phone, which I assume means you and Dog are watching something? What happened today?? Is it true that you set the science room on fire??

Write back asap.

J x

From: anna_huntley@zingmail.co.uk

To: jess.delby@zingmail.co.uk

Subject: Re: Are you a pyromaniac?!

Dad's out on a date so Dog and I are passing the time by YouTube-ing scenes from *The Lion King*. The reason I can't pick up the phone is because I attempted to lift Dog up as though he was Simba on Pride Rock during that "Circle of Life" song. Anyway, I couldn't do it and he fell back onto me, landing on my arm, which now really hurts and I think I twisted my ankle so I'm staying put on the sofa.

I think he's put on a few pounds.

No, I didn't set the science room on fire. I set Josie Graham's hair on fire.

Love, me xxx

From: jess.delby@zingmail.co.uk
To: anna_huntley@zingmail.co.uk
Subject: ARE YOU INSANE?!

Why would you set fire to Ms. Deputy Queen Bee's hair? You do realize that her mom once met Kate Moss? The school is really going to hate you, you know.

Is this because no one has asked you to the dance yet? Like some kind of protest thing against all the girls who have been asked? It's not until the end of semester–you've still got ages for someone to ask you.

J x

PS Why would you even think it was a good idea to try to lift a fully grown Labrador? Stop trying to act out movies, you weirdo.

From: anna_huntley@zingmail.co.uk
To: jess.delby@zingmail.co.uk
Subject: Re: ARE YOU INSANE?!

No, I am not insane. I just need to check that hair-spray-laden girls aren't anywhere near Bunsen burners when I turn them on in the future.

The school definitely hates me. Josie looked like she was going to strangle me or something. I feared for my life. It was like that time I peed myself a little bit when the really scary IT teacher at my last school yelled at me for taking paper out of the printer.

Do you think she'll tell Sophie? Do you think Sophie will hate me?

That would really be bad news because the

other day I could have sworn that Sophie laughed at one of my jokes she overheard me telling Danny in the hall. I thought that maybe she might not think I was such a loser after all. And, excuse me, but I don't even *care* that no one's asked me to the dance. I don't need a date. Last time I went to a dance I didn't have a date and I was totally fine. I just danced with a balloon. It made everyone laugh but in a "she's really funny" way not in a "laughing at me" way.

Love, me xxx

From: jess.delby@zingmail.co.uk
To: anna_huntley@zingmail.co.uk
Subject: Um . . . I'm sorry . . . what?

That e-mail was disturbing on so many levels.

You peed yourself? Dude, how old were you when this happened?

What do you mean you danced with a balloon? You're making me nervous with all these weird stories from your past.

J x

From: anna_huntley@zingmail.co.uk
To: jess.delby@zingmail.co.uk
Subject: Re: Um . . . I'm sorry . . . what?
It was two years ago. But only a little pee. It wasn't like I wet myself. She just came out of nowhere and it scared me.
Dancing with a balloon is a reasonable and funny thing to do. It's what Oscar Wilde would have done. It's a scathing comment on our society of dependent and irrational figures who consider themselves incomplete without a significant other.
Love, me xxx

From: jess.delby@zingmail.co.uk
To: anna_huntley@zingmail.co.uk
Subject: It is confirmed, you actually are insane
Maybe don't ever tell anyone else about that pee story.
Ditto the balloon one.
J x

From: anna_huntley@zingmail.co.uk
To: jess.delby@zingmail.co.uk

Subject: Quick question

Do you still want to be friends with me now that I've set Josie Graham's hair on fire?

I completely understand if you don't.

Same for Danny. If I were you guys I wouldn't want to be friends with me.

Love, me xxx

From: jess.delby@zingmail.co.uk

To: anna_huntley@zingmail.co.uk

Subject: Re: Quick question

Are you kidding? If we didn't have you as a friend, who would we laugh at?

We need you, if only for entertainment value.

J x

From: anna_huntley@zingmail.co.uk

To: jess.delby@zingmail.co.uk

Subject: Re: Quick question

Who did you laugh at before I came into your lives?

Love, me xxx

From: jess.delby@zingmail.co.uk

To: anna_huntley@zingmail.co.uk

Subject: Re: Quick question

The weirdo who used to live next door to Danny and sang songs from musicals while wearing a chicken suit.

I think the chicken suit was something to do with his job. Can't be sure.

Anyway, when he moved last summer, Danny and I were bummed. But then you totally filled that gap when you arrived in September.

J x

From: anna_huntley@zingmail.co.uk

To: jess.delby@zingmail.co.uk

Subject: Now I'm really depressed

Wait. I replaced a guy in a chicken suit who sang songs from Broadway shows?

THAT's WHO I REPLACED IN YOUR LIFE?

I should have set *myself* on fire today.

Love, me xxx

From: jess.delby@zingmail.co.uk
To: anna_huntley@zingmail.co.uk
Subject: Re: Now I'm really depressed
You know, if you really wanted to fill the gap left by the chicken-suit man, you could sing songs from musicals in lunch breaks.
My personal favorite is *Fame* because I'm fun and amazing. Danny's is *My Fair Lady* because he's basically an old man and apparently it's based on some play that no one cares about.
Just a tip if you really want to win us over.
J x

From: anna_huntley@zingmail.co.uk
To: jess.delby@zingmail.co.uk
Subject: HA
My stage career started and ended when I was forced to be a shepherd in a nativity play. I walked onto the stage, saw everyone staring, burst into tears, and ran straight back off. Into a tree.
Why, I have to ask, was there even a tree involved in the production? Last time I checked,

there were no trees in stables in Bethlehem.
Our drama teacher was clearly an idiot.
Also I can't sing. Not one note. Sorry to be a disappointment in comparison to chicken-suit man. So as much as I want to stay your friend for the rest of time, I can guarantee you—never going to happen.
I am, however, naturally gifted at setting people on fire.
Maybe my career lies in some kind of flame-inspired capacity. Ooh! Maybe I'll be really good at welding metal with blowtorches or something! THEN I COULD MAKE A SUIT JUST LIKE IRON MAN!
That would be so cool. I need to speak to our technology department. I'm guessing they'll have access to blowtorches? They need to take advantage of my skill set now while I'm young and malleable.
Love, me xxx

From: jess.delby@zingmail.co.uk
To: anna_huntley@zingmail.co.uk

Subject: Re: HA

What's Iron Man? Is it one of those Marvin comic book characters that you're obsessed with? Like that stretchy person?

J x

From: anna_huntley@zingmail.co.uk

To: jess.delby@zingmail.co.uk

Subject: Re: HA

Okay, firstly it's Marvel, not Marvin.

Secondly, please do not refer to Mr. Fantastic as "that stretchy person."

And lastly, yes, Iron Man is a comic book character. Tony Stark develops an iron suit with repulsor beams and flight ability so he can take on bad guys.

Everyone would want to be my friend if I had one of those!

Love, me xxx

From: jess.delby@zingmail.co.uk

To: anna_huntley@zingmail.co.uk

Subject: Re: HA

Now, you see, it's times like this when I genuinely worry that you're being serious.
J x

From: anna_huntley@zingmail.co.uk
To: jess.delby@zingmail.co.uk
Subject: Trust me
I am being serious.
I've just sent Dog on a mission to find Dad's tool kit. He might have something in there I can experiment with.
Love, me xxx

From: jess.delby@zingmail.co.uk
To: anna_huntley@zingmail.co.uk
Subject: You've lost it
You can't send dogs on missions. They can't understand what you're saying. They're DOGS.
Judging by today I think it might actually be best if you avoid any tools that produce flames.
What are you up to tonight, anyway? Let me guess . . . you've finished your homework

already (geek) and you're going to watch some film that was made before we were born (nerd).

Am I correct?

J x

From: anna_huntley@zingmail.co.uk
To: jess.delby@zingmail.co.uk
Subject: You're right

Pretty much. Dog came back with a lampshade instead of a tool kit. No idea where that came from. Anyway we are now watching this movie Dad is always going on about by that famous guy called Hitchcock. Bit of a slow start but Dad's recommendations are usually good. This one's meant to be a classic.

Love, me xxx

From: jess.delby@zingmail.co.uk
To: anna_huntley@zingmail.co.uk
Subject: IMPORTANT

What film have you put on, Anna? I mean it–this is important!

From: anna_huntley@zingmail.co.uk
To: jess.delby@zingmail.co.uk
Subject: Re: IMPORTANT
Chill out–it's called *Psycho*. Gotta go, it's starting.
Love, me xxx

From: jess.delby@zingmail.co.uk
To: anna_huntley@zingmail.co.uk
Subject: ABORT MISSION. MAYDAY. ABORT MISSION!
Anna–you do not want to watch that movie! I know what you're like with scary movies! It's a horror film!!! TURN IT OFF NOW.
You've turned it off, right?

From: jess.delby@zingmail.co.uk
To: anna_huntley@zingmail.co.uk
Subject: (no subject)
Anna? ANNA? Did you get my last e-mail???
That's it. I'm coming over. Don't build any forts this time.
J x

Hi, you have reached Nick Huntley's phone. Please leave your name, number, and any message, and I'll get back to you as soon as possible. Thank you.

BEEP

"Hi, Dad! Yeah, it's me. I know you're out and about, but I thought I'd call and say hi! And also tell you that I've decided to watch that *Psycho* movie you're always talking about. You know, the one by that director Hitchcock you're always giving long and boring speeches about. It was in the DVD player already, and Dog has settled right down so I know he approves. I hope this is entertaining. Enjoy your evening. Okay, bye."

Hi, you have reached Nick Huntley's phone. Please leave your name, number, and any message, and I'll get back to you as soon as possible. Thank you.

BEEP

"DAD! Dad, it's me. Dad, something awful has happened! Dad, she got stabbed. IN THE SHOWER. I can't BELIEVE that you let me watch something like that, that you actually ENCOURAGED me to watch that film. WHAT IS WRONG WITH YOU? I hope you know what this means. I WILL NEVER SHOWER AGAIN."

Hi, you have reached Nick Huntley's phone. Please leave your name, number, and any message, and I'll get back to you as soon as possible. Thank you.

BEEP

"Hey, Dad, so I was thinking. Maybe you could come home soon? Just quickly, you wouldn't have to miss anything. You could just come home, check the house for murderers, and then go back on out. Think about it. Okay, bye. OH MY GOD. THE DOORBELL JUST RANG. DAD, DAD, YOU HAVE TO COME HOME."

Hi, you have reached Nick Huntley's phone. Please leave your name, number, and any message, and I'll get back to you as soon as possible. Thank you.

BEEP

"Um, Mr. Huntley? Uh yeah, hi, this is Jess. You know, Anna's friend from school. Just to let you know that you can ignore all those messages she left you. I came over and found her in the closet, hiding behind the vacuum, holding your golf club. She's a bit better now though, so you don't need to worry. Lucky I know where your spare key is, hey? Anyway, hope you enjoy your evening. Uh yeah, bye."

JESS WAS WAITING BY MY LOCKER WHEN I CAME into school the next day.

"Morning, sunshine. How are you feeling?"

"Um," I replied, trying to ignore the glares of everyone passing us. "Not brilliant."

"I thought you might say that, which is why I bought you some of these." She reached into her bag and pulled out some gummy bears.

"Thanks, but I'm not sure even gummy bears can help this time."

"Look, don't worry about these guys," she said, gesturing to a group of sixth graders who giggled as they walked past. It looked like the whole school knew. "It will all blow over."

"I don't think it will somehow. I'm destined to be the girl who set Josie Graham on fire for the rest of my school career."

"Don't be silly. It was an accident; everyone knows that." Jess shrugged.

"Really?"

"Of course. Danny said he overheard Brendan Dakers saying it was an accident."

"What?" I said in utter shock. "Brendan Dakers said that? Are you sure?"

"Yes. Try not to swoon too much. It'll probably work in your favor, considering for some unknown reason people in this school tend to hang on his every word." She rolled her eyes. "Apparently he also said it was hilarious to watch."

"Something tells me that Josie won't have found it so funny." The first bell rang, and I sighed. "I wish I didn't have to go to class."

"Just laugh about it—no one was hurt." Jess gave me a friendly nudge. "It's like I said last night."

"Speaking of which, Dad wanted me to thank you again for coming over and rescuing me. Who knows how long I would have been in that closet for."

"No worries. Right, I better go, otherwise I'm going to be late, and I've already been given a warning about my tardiness." Jess swung her bag over her shoulder.

"Jess, you can't leave me. Sophie Parker is in this class.

She's going to kill me. You don't get away with setting fire to her best friend lightly."

"How could she kill you? She doesn't have any weapons."

"I'm not sure that would stop her."

"I think her sister had a black belt. She used to go to school here. She might have taught Sophie how to karate-chop you."

"A lot of saliva is building up in my mouth right now."

"Calm down. Sophie is not going to kill you. And if she was, then she would definitely wait until after school so as not to make it look suspicious."

"Great. Thanks for that."

"I hope she doesn't kill you."

"You're a good friend."

Jess gave me a cheerful wave and walked off into the direction of her class.

I stood there wishing I could be more like Jess. She's beautiful, super cool and confident, and never seems to worry about anything. She has long, blond dip-dyed hair and always paints her nails loads of different colors. She's good at every sport she plays and captain of the volleyball team, which made Sophie Parker really mad.

Sophie expected to be captain since she is pretty much in charge of everything else that goes on, being the most popular girl in our grade. Apparently her sister was the most popular girl in this school when she was here and was captain of all the sports teams. When Sophie wasn't appointed captain of the volleyball team, her parents were very upset about it and came in to speak to our PE teacher, while Sophie cried behind them.

Dad has never had this sort of problem with me. I peaked in physical education when I was eight and was forced to join a soccer activity at school. I was distracted by a pigeon, the ball came my way, deflected off my butt, and bounced into the goal. My sporting career has gone downhill ever since.

Anyway, Sophie dragging in her parents didn't faze our PE teacher, who stuck to her guns and told them Jess was captain, fair and square. Upsetting the most popular girl in our grade didn't exactly do much for Jess's popularity, but Jess got over that pretty quickly.

Our friendship was actually born that day, right after Sophie and her parents stormed out of the gym having not got their way. Jess was waiting for her best friend, Danny, and I was waiting for Dad to come to get me to pick up Mom from the airport (who came to stay for a week to see the new house and ask me unending questions about my first week at the new school).

We were standing in silence a few feet apart, and I noticed she looked pretty down. I guess because Sophie and her sidekick, Josie, had made it clear what they thought about Jess being made captain. I offered her a cookie, but she just shook her head in a "stop bugging me" way. I nodded, and we stood in silence again.

"You had a bad day?" I asked after a few minutes.

"Yeah." She sighed, folding her arms. "Pretty bad."

I was thoughtful for a moment. "Want me to do a tap dance for you?"

She blinked at me. "What?"

"To cheer you up. Here." I put my bag down and launched into what was not really a tap dance, because I've never done tap dancing and I wasn't wearing tap shoes. But it always made my dad laugh when I attempted it in our living room, so I thought it might go down well.

Jess watched me, baffled. And when Danny came along to walk home with her, I stopped. She didn't say anything but threw me a big smile over her shoulder as they left. The next day when I arrived at school, preparing for yet another terrifying morning of being the new girl no one was interested in, they both came over to me and asked if I needed showing around the place.

Ever since then Jess and Danny have really taken care of me at school. They showed me the ropes, like where to stand in assembly so you don't get spat on by over-enthusiastic teachers during announcements, and how to get the lunch ladies to give you second helpings.

Jess even picks me to be on her team in PE despite knowing I'm completely useless. I did tell her last semester that she didn't have to do that, and I wouldn't be insulted as I know I'm one of the worst.

"Whatever, Anna," she'd replied breezily. "It's not a pity thing. I like having you on my team. It's more of a challenge to win that way. And you know I love a challenge. Plus you provide excellent comic relief."

She can say what she likes—I know she picks me because she doesn't want me to be last.

Yep, it definitely would have been good right now to be Jess, but I wasn't. I was me. It stank. I walked into class apprehensively, noticed that the room hushed, and went to sit down in my chair. Immediately a shadow fell over my desk, and I blinked up to see Sophie Parker staring down at me with her arms folded, her light gray eyes narrowing at me, and her glossy highlighted hair falling neatly around her shoulders.

"Hannah, isn't it?" she said.

"Um. Anna."

"Right. Jess Delby's best friend."

Uh-oh.

"So I heard about what happened yesterday, obviously. What you tried to do to *my* best friend. What is wrong with you? You could have really hurt her."

"Don't exaggerate, Sophie. Josie had her hair singed and that was it," a voice piped up from the corner.

Sophie spun around to see who had dared defy her, and Connor Lawrence, leaning back in his chair looking very pleased with himself, stared right back at her mischievously through his dark bangs.

Great. I groaned inwardly. Of all the people to come to my defense, it had to be someone like Connor Lawrence. He has fewer friends than me. And I only have two. (Three if you count Dog, but Jess and Danny say that I can't, which personally I find unreasonable.)

"Um, who even *are* you?"

My heart sank as Connor ignored Sophie entirely and went on. "If Josie had any brains, she would have just turned on the faucet right next to where she was sitting and shoved her big head under it."

There was a nervous titter around the classroom, and I

felt the tension rising rapidly as Sophie inhaled sharply at the insult to her sidekick. I sat awkwardly, wishing that Connor would just leave it alone.

"Ugh. Don't even bother speaking to me. No one asked you your opinion, weirdo!" Sophie spat angrily before turning toward me again. "Did you set fires at your last school? Is that why you don't have any friends?"

"No, no, of course not. It was—"

"Sit down, Sophie. It was an accident."

I turned in shock because this time it wasn't just anyone speaking up. Too cool to even look up from his phone while speaking, it was Brendan Dakers. *Brendan Dakers.* The most popular and best-looking boy in my class, possibly in the entire school. And captain of the soccer and rugby teams. He is also really smart and always gets the best grades. Basically, he's the perfect male specimen. Every time I look at him, my feet go tingly.

I've never really spoken to him. He's way too popular. Of course, Sophie Parker and Josie Graham are always hanging around him. In fact Sophie and Brendan are sort of an unofficial couple. They aren't actually together, but they should be. Everyone knows it's going to happen one day. Probably at the dance.

They're both really beautiful. If they ever reproduced (ew), their children would be another level of human—superhuman. Jess disagrees with me on this and says that if they ever had children, they might get Brendan's looks and Sophie's personality, which would make them vampires.

I'm not sure of the logic in this, but I'm not sure that Jess's brain works in a logical way.

I don't know how either Jess or Sophie manage to remain collected in his presence. If Brendan Dakers ever spoke to me, I would be so ecstatic I would probably die. Which would be an excellent way to go.

Sadly, the chances of Brendan speaking to me are nil for the following reasons:

1. When I first saw him I choked on my own spit.
2. When he once walked past our volleyball lesson and waved to Sophie, I had a moment of complete deliriousness and thought he was waving at me. When I waved back, he looked puzzled. Probably because we had never spoken before, and I don't think he even knew I was in his grade at that point. I'm not even sure he realizes that now.

3. When I mistakenly waved back at Brendan Dakers in volleyball, Josie Graham said really loudly to Sophie, "That is *so* mortifying for her!" and they both burst out laughing. He witnessed this.
4. I set his friend Josie on fire.

Reflecting on this list has made me wonder how I even have two friends.

"Brendan, Josie's hair went up in flames," Sophie snapped.

"Relax," Brendan said, looking up from his phone briefly. "It was funny."

And with that, he went back to playing on his phone. The room silently watched Sophie's reaction. Her cheeks flushed with anger, and she gave me one last dramatic huff before pulling her shoulders back and stalking to her desk.

Someone snorted from the back of the classroom. It sounded like Connor. To my great relief Sophie didn't appear to have heard and flung herself into her chair, pulling out her fluffy purple pencil case just as Mr. Avery strolled in with his coffee and asked us to turn to page fifty-six.

I was so caught up in replaying Brendan Dakers sticking

up for me—sort of—over and over in my head that I didn't even hear the bell ring. It was only when I noticed people actually walking out of the classroom that I realized it was time for the next class and started to pack up my things in a hurry.

Brendan finding Josie being set on fire funny still didn't mean that Sophie had decided to let it go with me. As I got up, I accidentally nudged Sophie, who had been walking toward the door.

"Urgh!" she exhaled in exasperation, probably at the idea of me touching her, and looked at me in disgust as I hurriedly got out of her way.

Then she shook her head, swished back her perfect hair, and practically skipped toward Brendan, who, unlike me, clearly *had* been forgiven for the classroom standoff and was waiting for her by the door.

I finished packing up my stuff and began to make my way out too.

"Chin up, Ms. Huntley," Mr. Avery said cheerily as he took time out from wiping the board to look at me with sympathy. "You'll make friends here eventually. Sometimes it takes a while to find your feet. I remember having no friends whatsoever for a good few semesters at my middle school."

"Oh, well"—I stopped by the door—"thanks but I do have *some* friends here."

"Do you?" he said, looking surprised. "Splendid!"

Then he got back to wiping the board.

Sometimes I really wish I was a hermit. Not only do they not have to deal with people in general, but they're also usually very wise. I can only aspire to that state of being.

5.

THE SCHOOL DANCE STRESSES ME OUT. AND IT'S NOT because I won't have a date.

It is actually because school dances highlight the dictation of a dominating society on a youthful generation to locate a suitable partner of similar social standing with whom to spend the evening, not based on intellectual or personality compatibility, but on visual attraction alone. School dances are a staple of the dominant ideology in which we live, serving only the interest of a certain elite platform of students to exert their superiority and their peer influence, thus maintaining the existing state of the school's social context.

OKAY, FINE, it's because I'll never find a date.

Ever since the semester started, everyone has been talking about this Beatus dance, which takes place at the end of the spring semester. It's for grades six to eight and apparently is kind of like a smaller version of the prom.

"What on earth is the Betty dance?" I'd asked Jess one afternoon when I overheard for the third time that day someone in the bathroom talking about who was going to be elected for the committee.

"It's the Beatus dance, you mongoose." Jess laughed.

"It means 'blessed' or 'fortunate' in Medieval Latin, Anna," Danny explained gently, giving Jess a shove. This was typical Danny behavior, always on hand to remind Jess when to be a little more patient.

I once told him that I thought he was probably one of the nicest people I had ever met. "And your hair complements that." I smiled.

"Huh?" He automatically ran a hand through his thick blond curls that really are spectacular.

"I think when it comes to you, Danny," I'd said matter-of-factly, "your hair reflects your kindness and comforting nature."

That didn't actually go down too well. It turns out boys don't really strive to be kind and comforting. Danny, Jess had informed me after he'd left grumpily, gets tired of always being "the nice one" who girls want to be friends with.

The very next day after the curls comment I made sure to say, immediately as he walked in, "Danny! You look very rugged today. I think it's the way you're carrying your backpack on one shoulder." I ignored the muffled snigger of Jess next to me and continued with the confidence boost. "Seriously, something very manly going on there."

He looked surprised—but I've noticed he's carried his backpack on one shoulder ever since.

"It used to be called the spring dance for lower grades," Danny had continued.

Meanwhile Jess smiled at me and muttered, "Betty dance. Honestly!" under her breath.

"Our last principal picked the name because, as she continually reminded us, the lower grades were very lucky to have a dance at all when most schools just have a senior dance."

"She had to give it a Latin name to try to make it sound boring and educational." Jess grinned.

"Sounds fun to me."

"Not really." Jess shrugged. "It's really just an excuse for people like Sophie Parker to show off."

"Oh come on." Danny laughed. "You had a good time last year."

"The highlight was when you fell over on the dance floor."

"I did not fall over," Danny protested, going bright red. "I was doing the worm."

"Do you go with a . . . date?" I asked timidly, pretending not to really care.

"Most people do. Danny and I just went together." Jess sighed. "Although I pretended I didn't know him when he fell over."

"I told you, I was doing the worm!"

"It didn't look like the worm. It looked like you fell over and had hurt your hip or something."

I had worried about the dance all during Christmas vacation. If Jess and Danny were going to go together again, who would I go with? They weren't going to want a tagalong.

Now that I've set a girl on fire, I don't think my chances of getting a date are much improved.

I did consider putting a bow tie on Dog and going down the comedy route, but then I decided that I should play it safe, and if I was going to bring anyone they should probably be human.

Sophie Parker and Josie Graham are representing our grade on the Beatus committee of course. This means that they have to give up some of their lunch breaks to stand behind a table and sell raffle tickets to try to raise money for the dance budget. The prize is a two-week internship over spring break with Brendan's mom, who is a photographer.

"Your dad should have offered an internship," Jess commented, as we watched Sophie and Josie giggle with some other pretty girls in our grade who were buying plenty of tickets each. "Everyone would have bought tickets then, not just the school's princess contingent."

I snorted. "Sadly you exaggerate. I hardly think anyone at this school is interested in tanks."

"Whatever—he interviews celebrities all the time."

"I guess." I shrugged. "Most of the time he just sits at home yelling about writer's block and standing still with his forehead against the wall. He says it helps him think. He can stand there for about half an hour. Once I stood with him with my forehead against the wall to see what happened. I got no inspiration whatsoever. We both just stood there in silence with our heads touching the wall until I finally got hungry and left him to it. Not sure an intern would be a good idea."

"They're so embarrassing." Jess shook her head as Josie took out a pocket mirror and admired herself. "I bet Sophie has already bought half the tickets. The idea of getting in there with Brendan's family will be the only thing she cares about. She couldn't care less about the internship."

"Why don't you buy a raffle ticket? You're pretty good at photography."

Jess burst out laughing. "Yeah, on my camera phone. Not sure that counts."

"Go on, it's only a dollar a ticket, and if you win, I bet you'd get to go on some cool fashion shoots too. You'd be great!"

I wasn't lying. Jess *is* good at photography; she has a framed photo on her wall at home that she won a competition with when she was younger. Plus she is artistic too; her mom has shown me some of her paintings.

I made sure that when Jess came over to my house for the first time, Dad hid my pottery attempts that he usually displays on the mantel. Not proudly, he always likes to tease me, but because they are excellent conversation starters. I don't protest this. My Christmas robin is quite literally a blob of clay with a red circle in the middle.

"Anna." Jess sighed. "They won't be looking for someone like me, will they? I'm sure Brendan's mom will be much happier with someone like Sophie who can hang on to her every word and look the part."

"You look the perfect part," I said sharply. "Come on; if you don't get one, then I'll buy one for you."

She finally gave in to my pestering, and we made our way over to the table. Sophie saw us approaching and nudged Josie in the ribs, who looked up and immediately scowled.

"What do you want?" she spat, folding her arms.

"I'm so sorry about chemistry, Josie," I squeaked, feeling genuinely bad. "If there's anything I can do—"

"Personally," Jess interrupted chirpily, "I think your hair looks much better that length, Josie."

"That hardly makes things okay," Sophie replied angrily, tilting her head.

"Yes." Josie pouted, taking her cue as ever from Queen Sophie. "There's nothing you can do about it now."

"Great, glad that's all sorted," Jess said firmly. "Now, I'd like to buy a raffle ticket please."

Sophie's mouth dropped open. "You. *You* would like to buy a raffle ticket."

"Yes, one please."

"But"—Josie sniggered, looking her up and down—"you clearly don't care about . . . the way things look."

Jess's cheeks started to go red.

"I'm not really sure it's your thing, Jess," Sophie said with a tone of mock regret and then shrugged. "I wouldn't bother buying a ticket. It's *professional* photography."

Jess looked at the ground, embarrassed, and I'm really not quite sure what came over me, but suddenly words were coming out of my mouth.

"Ten tickets please."

They all stared at me in shock. "Yeah, ten." I repeated in a squeakier tone than I would have liked. I reached into my purse and held out the money.

Sophie snorted and Josie followed suit, but there was now a small line beginning to form behind me. Josie looked at Sophie for instruction. Sophie pursed her lips and gave a curt nod. Josie snatched the money and shoved the tickets across the table.

I walked away triumphantly, my heart slamming against my chest.

"Well, what do you know." Jess grinned as I passed her the tickets. She gave me a small grateful nudge. "Thanks."

Sitting in French later that afternoon, I couldn't stop thinking about the Beatus dance. What would happen if they didn't let me in because I didn't have a date? Even worse, what would happen if they did let me in, but then everyone was dancing in pairs and I was the ONLY one not dancing?! What would happen if everyone started pointing and laughing at me because I was so pathetic?! WHAT WOULD HAPPEN IF I GENUINELY DID HAVE TO BRING DOG AS MY DATE?!

This called for emergency note passing with Jess.

Hey—can I ask you a question?

Anna, you're passing notes in French? Are you crazy?! She'll catch us! Ms. Brockley is very smart—she does archery in her spare time.

It's important.

Okay, go on then, ask away.

Would you date me?

What?

If you were a boy, would you date me?

This is uncomfortable.

No it's not. I need to know.

Well I don't know. Probably not.

WHAT? WHY NOT?

Because of your obsession with your dog. He's cute and everything but you're out of control.

Do I talk about Dog a lot?

Yes. But maybe not so much around boys so they might not know about the obsession, which is a good thing. You could keep it under wraps until you marry the guy and then, BOOM. Let out the truth about your weirdness.

Oh. Okay.

Why does it bother you so much that you don't have a date? It's just a dance. Who cares?

It is not just a dance. Everyone is talking about it. And it's only the beginning of the semester so it will get worse leading up to it.

I don't have a date.

You have Danny. And anyway you CHOOSE not to have a date. I bet every boy in our grade would do anything to be your date to the Beatus dance.

You have Danny too. We'll go as a trio.

What about the slow dances?

What ABOUT the slow dances?

We can't dance as a trio!

Why not?

BECAUSE. That would look weird. How would you even do that?

We could all hold hands in a circle and sway.

Like some kind of cult? I don't think that would go over very well.

We could chant too.

I can tell you're making fun of me now. I don't

know whether you've noticed but I am actually being serious.

Why do you get so worked up about stupid things like this? It's a DANCE. Only people like Sophie get worked up about stupid things like this.

People like Sophie never get worked up about things like this. They don't need to. She doesn't need to ever worry about having a date. I bet she's going with Brendan Dakers.

Word on the street is that he hasn't asked her. Anyway, forget about Queen Sophie. Why don't you take Dog as your date?

Ha! Jess, you really do have the most bizarre brain! As if that would even occur to me as an idea!

You considered it, didn't you?

What?! You're ridiculous. Of course I did not consider taking Dog as my date to the Beatus dance.

You thought about putting a bow tie on him, didn't you?

This conversation is neither here nor there. Stop passing me notes please. Ms. Brockley is coming this way and I already have detention for a whole semester.

I think there are lots of people out there who would date you.

Really? You do?

Lesson number one about making friends and finding a date for the dance: play it cool. Seriously.

Got it. Should I write this down??

I was mocking you.

Oh. You should be clearer about things like that.

I'm going to go away now.

Okay! We can chat after class.

You have detention, dummy. E-mail me when you're home. Oh and, Anna?

Yes?

The only reason you wouldn't be able to find a date to the dance is because no one in this school is good enough.

Are you mocking me again?

No.

How can I tell?

By asking me. I just told you I wasn't mocking you.

That was a very nice thing for you to say! Like seriously nice. Like a true best friend thing to say! You never say nice things!

Don't be embarrassing.

I'm keeping that note forever.

Don't do that.

I'm going to stick it in my diary. I don't have a diary but I'm going to buy one ESPECIALLY so I can stick that note in it. And draw hearts around it.

Stop this.

And then one day I'll blow it up into a poster and frame it.

I would not put any of this past you. Leave me alone now. I'm not passing any more notes.

Fare thee well, Jess! You are a true and wonderful friend who believes in me. I will spread your kindness far and wide. You have brought hope and love to a troubled soul. Bless you and your people.

I strongly dislike you.

6.

ANNA HUNTLEY's LIFE GOALS

Compiled with personal commentary in day one of detention
Spring term 2015

1. Be a better person.

I will try to be nicer to people, like Dad, even when he's being really annoying. And I will start doing nice things like talk to strangers on the street or something. I can ask them about their day and their ambitions in life. Although I will try to do this without coming across like a crazy person, like that woman on the bus who yells hello at everyone who gets on and actually just scares people. But I'm sure she's just being nice.

2. Go to Africa and hand out rice.
I've been lucky in life to have a wonderful family (even if they are annoying a lot of the time) and wonderful friends (even though there are only two of them). Therefore, it is only right that I should give something back to the world. I'm sure they always need people to go to Africa and do good things like hand out rice. Note to self: search for charities online that organize trips to do good things like hand out rice.

"What are you writing?"

I frowned. I could tell that Connor Lawrence had been trying to see what I was writing ever since I got out my pen. He had strolled in late to detention—who is this carefree?!—and sat down next to me without bothering to take his headphones off.

"Nice of you to join us, Connor," Mr. Kenton had sniffed, not looking particularly bothered about it.

"Nothing," I whispered back, trying to cover my notepad.

"Looks like a list."

"It's not a list."

"I can see it's a list."

"Fine. It's a list."

"What is the list of?"

"Are you always this nosy?" I asked, trying not to sound too defensive, but at the same time wanting him to leave me alone. This, after all, was the person who'd escalated Sophie's annoyance at me about sending Josie into a full-on tantrum for the whole class to witness.

"I'm interested," he replied, smugly.

"It's nothing important."

"What does it say at the top?"

"It says you're going to get us in trouble."

"Funny." We both looked up at Mr. Kenton. His head was hanging down, and his eyes were closed. A faint snore came from his direction.

Connor grinned. "I think we're safe."

I gave him an "end of discussion" look and went back to my list.

3. Find a date for the Beatus dance—the ideal would be Brendan Dakers but clearly, at this point, anyone would be an achievement.
There will be more chance of this happening if I achieve point 1. Brendan Dakers isn't going to be interested in someone who is not kind and thoughtful.

Also he will probably be impressed by someone with cool skills (see point 5 below to nail this one) and by someone who is not a disaster and talks about interesting things (for example, their recent trip to Africa to hand out rice to those in need).

4. Meet comic book world GOD, Stan Lee, and inspire a great comic strip about a girl keeping London safe from the threat of evil.
Should this ever happen I will be content for the rest of my days and never complain about one single thing AGAIN. I promise not to say anything embarrassing to the man who created some of the best characters in the world. Note to self: Does asking him to make me into a comic book superhero count as embarrassing? Confer with Jess.

5. Learn how to do hip-hop dancing.
A necessary skill in life. Bound to impress pretty much everyone anywhere. Handy to pull out in an awkward or sad situation to make things better. Your friend just got dumped? Pull out the running man! Lost your homework the day it's due? Wait a

second, let me pull out the running man! Hate your life? So does everyone! Pull out the running man!

6. Save someone's life.
Preferably on land and not in the sea because I hate seaweed and jellyfish.

"Wait, you know who Stan Lee is?"

I whipped my head up. "Hey!"

"What? It's not like you're covering it very well." Connor shrugged. "Go on, let me have a look."

"I didn't want you to see," I complained. "How would you like it if I just leaned over and looked at your work?"

"Feel free." He slid his notepad along the desk to the edge. "You might actually appreciate it."

I glanced at the open page and then pulled it closer to gaze down in awe. The notepad was littered with animation sketches. "You drew these? They're good."

"Thanks. I'm thinking of doing my own graphic novel some day. I approve of point four. Personally I've always thought Batman the best creation of all time." He pulled his notebook away from my gaze.

"Please, Batman? He's amazing, but Marvel has SO many

cooler heroes. Look at Spider-Man, for example."

He raised an eyebrow. "I'm not going to take that seriously from someone who has learning to hip-hop dance higher on their list than saving someone's life."

"Who said these were in order of importance?" Before he spotted point 3, I put a protective arm round my notebook and changed the subject. "Who would your superhero be?"

"Sorry?"

"In your comic?"

"I'm waiting for inspiration." He grinned. "But me probably."

"How original."

"I'd have to come up with a superpower." He looked thoughtful. "What would yours be?"

"It would be cool to control things with my mind, like Jean Grey in X-Men," I replied. "Before she was taken over by the Phoenix Force and became evil, obviously."

"Obviously," Connor agreed.

"Also," I added, noticing him straighten up to try and peer over my arm that was hiding what I'd written, "controlling things with my mind would mean I could make you STOP LOOKING AT MY LIST!"

Mr. Kenton grunted and shifted in his seat. I narrowed my eyes at Connor and continued.

7. Get over fear of pigeons.
Ugh, the flapping. Plus it is becoming increasingly difficult to live in London with this phobia.

8. Invent something useful for mankind.
So that I can be thought of as charitable and helpful at the same time. Like the clever person who invented that spray balsamic vinegar so that it doesn't spill all over your plate and ruin your salad.

"What about a pigeon-deflecting helmet?"

"Excuse me?"

Connor was leaning back in his chair with a pen in his mouth. "That covers points seven and eight."

"No, it doesn't. Putting on a deflecting helmet wouldn't cure my fear of pigeons. It would just keep them away from me." I sighed. "Don't assume I didn't already think about that one."

9. Have name engraved on a trophy.
Unlikely to be for a sporting event so may have to think outside the box for this one. Do they give out trophies to people who hand out rice in Africa? (Note to self: research this.)

10. Train Dog to high five.
It took him ten months to learn that his name was Dog. This is probably the most ambitious life goal on this list.

When detention finally ended, I stowed my list away safely into my bag and filed out of the classroom with everyone else toward the main school doors, ready for freedom.

"Hey! Spidey!" Connor was suddenly at my side. "Did you finish your list? When does the world get to witness the hip-hop dancing? I'm gripped with anticipation."

I snorted. "Uh. Never? Forget the list; it is PERSONAL."

"All right, all right." He grinned as he opened the exit door for me, and I marched past him. "Don't get your Spidey senses in a twist."

"Okay," I grumbled at him, stomping down the steps. "Just because I admire the superior skills of Spider-Man does not mean that—"

"That you know anything about comics? Don't sweat it."

"Hey!" I held out my arm to stop him in his tracks as we walked out of the gates. "Do not insult my comic knowledge. I could take you on in a Marvel or DC face-off any time."

"If you say so." He smiled broadly.

"Good," I said huffily, and continued through the gates on to the road. "See you tomorrow then."

"Hey, Anna. Just so you know, about point three on that personal list I definitely didn't see, I reckon you should have higher standards when it comes to the ideal person to take you on a date."

My mouth dropped open.

"But as I say"—he swung his bag over his shoulder with a mischievous grin—"I definitely didn't see anything. See you tomorrow, Spidey."

He strolled off down the road and left me standing on my own, my mouth still hanging open.

Note to self: stop writing lists.

From: jess.delby@zingmail.co.uk
To: anna_huntley@zingmail.co.uk
Subject: Come on

Are you home yet? I'm bored.

How was detention? I can't believe you did something as selfish as set someone on fire. Now you have detention so I have no one to distract me from this French vocab.

Danny is so annoying. He purposefully doesn't

reply to my e-mails so that I'm forced to do my homework.

J x

From: anna_huntley@zingmail.co.uk
To: jess.delby@zingmail.co.uk
Subject: Re: Come on

Hey, I'm home!

Get this–Dad took Dog to the vet today for his annual checkup. Do you know what this so-called vet had to say? That Dog was "healthy."

Can you believe that?! I am tempted to march right up to that vet and give him a piece of my mind!

Have you had dinner, by the way?

Love, me xxx

From: jess.delby@zingmail.co.uk
To: anna_huntley@zingmail.co.uk
Subject: Re: Come on

I'm confused. Isn't being healthy a good thing for a dog?

I did have dinner, yes. You are full of interesting questions. We had spaghetti.
Do what you will with this information.
J x

From: anna_huntley@zingmail.co.uk
To: jess.delby@zingmail.co.uk
Subject: Poor Dog
It is fine for a dog to be healthy, Jess, but it is not fine for a stranger to call Dog "healthy." Do you get it now?
I was actually going to ask if you wanted to come over here for dinner so you could jump in and save me if Dad tried to lecture me about the importance of bumblebees or something.
So there.
Love, me xxx

From: jess.delby@zingmail.co.uk
To: anna_huntley@zingmail.co.uk
Subject: Re: Poor Dog
No, I do not get it now. Nobody would get it

now. You're not making any sense.

Very kind of you, want me to come over anyway? I could distract your dad with questions about military arms.

J x

From: anna_huntley@zingmail.co.uk
To: jess.delby@zingmail.co.uk
Subject: Re: Poor Dog

He was clearly referring to Dog's size.

Love, me xxx

From: jess.delby@zingmail.co.uk
To: anna_huntley@zingmail.co.uk
Subject: You're crazy

Again. That is a GOOD thing. That he is HEALTHY.

Am I coming over?

J x

From: anna_huntley@zingmail.co.uk
To: jess.delby@zingmail.co.uk
Subject: Re: You're crazy

Hang on. Better not come over yet.
Dad wants me to log off. He wants to "have a talk" about something "very important." He's been acting so weird the past few days.
Anyway I'll be back on in about half an hour and will let you know.
Love, me xxx

From: jess.delby@zingmail.co.uk
To: anna_huntley@zingmail.co.uk
Subject: Leave me why don't you
Hope everything is okay. Let me know?
J x

From: jess.delby@zingmail.co.uk
To: anna_huntley@zingmail.co.uk
Subject: You there?
Hey, Anna–just wondering what your dad had to say? It's been a couple of hours so checking everything is okay.
Plus, I'm really bored. Why is there so much vocab in the French language? Surely we don't need to know this much if we ever go

over there, right? We'd only need to know "croissant" and "non" to get by, I'm pretty sure of it.

So why am I learning the French translation of "antler"?

When am I going to be in France talking about antlers? Our school is so strange.

J x

From: jess.delby@zingmail.co.uk

To: anna_huntley@zingmail.co.uk

Subject: (no subject)

Me again! It's been a while now–what's going on? Is everything all right with your dad?

I'm worried.

J x

From: jess.delby@zingmail.co.uk

To: anna_huntley@zingmail.co.uk

Subject: (no subject)

I haven't heard from you all night.

Something's happened, hasn't it?

WHAT IN THE WORLD HAS HAPPENED?

MY DAD HAS COMPLETELY LOST HIS MIND.

I knew something was wrong earlier this evening because he was acting all shifty. I couldn't think of anything that might be bugging him, so I asked him whether Mrs. Trott had got into our trash can again.

Mrs. Trott is our next-door neighbor who, when we first moved in, clearly had a bit of a thing for Dad. Unfortunately, she has quite a mean scary face, and Dad didn't reciprocate Mrs. Trott's amorous advances. After this, she has become very intently focused on our recycling in what appears to me to be an admirable attempt at crossing Dad's path more regularly.

One day I came home to find Dad a nervous wreck. It turned out that in a fit of passion over Dad's refusal to comply with her previous instruction, she had got into our trash can.

So when Dad took the trash out of the house and opened the lid to the outside can, there was Mrs. Trott's scary face staring right up at him.

According to witnesses, Dad had "screamed at an impressive pitch" and then fallen backward over his pile of trash bags. Mrs. Trott, I was told, calmly climbed out of the can and simply said, "Recycle, you fool," then threw a last lingering look over her shoulder.

Dad has recycled meticulously since.

"No, Mrs. Trott wasn't in our trash can. Why?" Dad replied, looking up in a panic. "I've been so careful!"

"Calm down, Dad," I said in my most reassuring voice. "Mrs. Trott has been extremely pleased with your recycling recently." He looked visibly calmer. "But why are you acting so weird? You're creeping me out."

Then he said, all defensive, "I'm not acting weird," and started tidying the phone table. I watched him for a minute and then got bored, shrugged, and left him to be abnormal on his own.

So when he came into the living room and made me turn off my laptop, I was kind of relieved because I could finally find out what had been going on.

He sat down next to me and took a deep breath. "I have asked my . . . um . . . girlfriend to come over to meet you this evening. I hope that's all right?"

"Oh right! Uh, yeah, of course that's fine."

"There is something I just want to explain to you first."

He gave me a funny look.

"This girlfriend is . . . unique." He stopped and clamped his hands together in front of him, leaning forward. "She is special."

"Okay, Dad, I get it. This one's different. Don't worry, I'll be on my best behavior. I promise I won't tell her that story about when you angered that ostrich."

"That's very kind of you, but that's actually not what I meant."

"Okay," I said, rolling my eyes. Now I got it. "It's because she's really young, isn't it? If that is the case, you definitely don't need to worry. You have really good hair for your age. Unless she's early twenties or something, in which case I'm sorry, but you both need to re-evaluate your lives."

"No, look, she's my age, she's fine. It's just . . ." He took a deep breath. "Anna, my girlfriend is Helena Montaine."

I blinked at him.

"Helena Montaine," I repeated slowly.

"As in . . . the actress," he confirmed, looking at me intently. "As in the really famous actress."

"Yes."

"As in the really famous two-time Oscar-winning actress."

"Yes."

"You're dating Helena Montaine, the actress?"

"Yes."

"Helena Montaine, the famous actress, is dating my dad?"

"Yes."

"Is this a weird joke?"

"No."

"You're not in cahoots with Jess?"

"No. I am being serious."

"Because this is the sort of thing she would do."

"No, I'm not in cahoots with Jessica."

"You're dating Helena Montaine, the actress who's always in the newspapers."

"Yes."

"The famous one."

"Yes."

I sat in silence. I wasn't sure how to process this information. I mean, it's not like Dad hasn't dated famous people before. He dated a fairly high-profile politician for a bit and even once went on a few dates with a model he'd interviewed.

Not that any of them had ever taken any notice of me of course. I'm the least glamorous being they probably ever had contact with, apart from Dog maybe. But even he can look like a big shot after a good groom.

Helena Montaine is *big* though. As in famous. Really famous. She is always on the front covers of all those glossy magazines that my dad won't let me read because they "encourage things like more eyeliner requests." (Seriously, he needs to get out more.)

She's even advertised skin products on television. You know the ones, where she's running along a beach in a white floaty dress and touching her face because it's so soft and wrinkle-free.

"Are you all right, Anna?" My dad looked extremely worried and even reached out for my hand.

"Um," I said, trying to get past the images of Helena stroking her face and saying "so silky, so you" flashing through my mind.

"Look, it's important that you know how normal she is. I was nervous when I first interviewed her because I assumed she would be a diva. But she's extremely approachable and down to earth."

"Right," I said numbly.

"You have to think of it as just meeting your dad's girlfriend rather than meeting Helena Montaine. I promise, once you've met her, you'll forget all that famous nonsense right away. She has a way of putting you perfectly at ease."

"You interviewed her. That's how you met?"

"Yes. I had to interview her a couple of times because she had such a hectic schedule. We couldn't do the interview all in one go. But every time I saw her after that first interview it was like we were old friends. We clicked right away. After I wrote the piece, I asked her if she'd like to go for a drink some time, and well . . ." He paused and gave a shrug. "It all started from there."

"And now you're her . . . boyfriend?"

"Yes."

"She knows about the tanks book?"

"Yes."

"And she still wants to date you? Helena Montaine, the famous actress, is dating my dad, the author of a tanks book."

"I have done more with my life than just write a book about tanks. Not that that's the point here."

"I'm about to meet Helena Montaine."

"Yes. It's difficult to digest, but she'll be here any minute, and you can see how wonderful she is. I also invited Marianne—you know Helena has a daughter?—as I've met her a few times now. She's very nice, Anna, a really lovely girl. We thought it would be good for you guys to get to know each other. Marianne is only seventeen, so there's not much of an age difference between you. I know you'll get along wonderfully. She's a little high maintenance but it's mostly for show—I think."

Dad may have all his hair, but he seems to have lost several of his brain cells along the way. Marianne Montaine and me get along? IS HE NUTS?! She is a movie star's daughter who doesn't have an actual job but is so beautiful and glamorous that she gets invited to every red carpet event anyway. Whereas I can recite *Lord of the Rings* passages and spend weekends re-enacting the climbing of Mount Doom scene with my Labrador.

She has a Wikipedia page for goodness' sake! I once got left off the school registery at the start of the new year. MY OWN SCHOOL DIDN'T REMEMBER ME.

The doorbell rang. I looked at Dad. Dad looked at me. My eye twitched.

"Anna . . . ," he warned. I feigned innocence.

Then without a moment's warning I leaped to my feet. Dad was clearly prepared and jumped up at the same time.

The race was on.

I ran full speed toward the stairs with Dad in hot pursuit. As I went to jump two steps at a time, he propelled himself forward and gripped my right ankle. I fell flat on the stairs, desperately trying to drag myself up while shaking my right leg manically in the hope of loosening his iron grip.

"Anastasia Huntley! Stop . . . this . . . now!" Dad said through gritted teeth.

"You . . . stop . . . this . . . now!" I retorted, trying to reach for the banister to get some kind of grip. I flung my leg from side to side, but he held tight, determined to reign victorious in our grapple.

Gradually he managed to slide me down the stairs until, with a last yank on my ankle, I slumped to the floor, my chin bumping each step as I went. Dad sat next to me, leaning against the wall and out of breath.

The doorbell rang again. He got to his feet, turned to me as I rolled over onto my back, said, "Right, I'll go let them in," gave me a thumbs-up, and went to open the door.

I was still lying awkwardly on the stairs in a contorted

starfish position when Helena and Marianne Montaine breezed through the door and Dad gave them both a warm welcome. They looked a little surprised as I stood up awkwardly from the stairs and brushed myself down.

"Um," Dad began, glancing at me. "This is my daughter, Anna."

"Hello." I nodded and then curtseyed.

I CURTSEYED.

Dad closed his eyes in exasperation. Marianne Montaine looked at her mother in utter bafflement. Helena Montaine glanced at Dad and then took a step forward and curtseyed too. "Lovely to meet you, Anna."

"Let's all go into the living room, shall we?" Dad laughed *very* nervously and ushered us in.

It was completely surreal. I found myself standing stiffly in my living room with Helena and Marianne Montaine. And I'll tell you something: all it takes is a Hollywood film star and an It Girl standing in front of you to become exceedingly aware of how unacceptable it is to go into society every day looking like yourself.

Helena was exactly as a film star should be. Tall and elegant, she was dressed in a white pantsuit with a chunky gold necklace and matching earrings. Those face products must be working, because her skin was glowing as she looked down at me with a bright smile.

Marianne has the same delicate features as her mother, the big blue eyes and slightly pronounced mouth. Her brown hair was impossibly glossy and, wearing a short blue minidress with a leather jacket and sunglasses perched on the top of her head, biker boots, and sporting plenty of black eyeliner, she looked every inch the rock star's daughter.

Which, incidentally, she is, as Helena's first husband, and the father of her only child, was one fifth of a rock band in the seventies. There was no mistaking the brief up-and-down glance she gave me as she took in my appearance.

I wanted to die. There was no way I was ever going to forgive my dad for this one. He could at least have given me a moment to attempt to make my hair look presentable before their arrival.

Although maybe he thought that since I hadn't managed to make my hair ever look acceptable in the past twelve years, ten more minutes probably wasn't going to help.

"It's so lovely to have you both here, Helena and Marianne," Dad announced, clapping his hands together.

"It's lovely to be here." Helena smiled her impeccably white-toothed smile at him, and he stared dopily at her.

Gross.

Helena nudged her daughter subtly. "Thank you for having us," Marianne added quietly, looking at Dad. Dad then looked at me.

I'm not sure what he was expecting. I assume he hoped I might follow suit and take my turn graciously to announce how "lovely" it was to have them. To his disappointment, my brain was still not fully functioning.

"My chin is not normally this red," I began.

The three of them stared at me.

"Yeah," I continued when no one replied. "I had an incident on the stairs."

I thought about launching into an explanation, but I decided I had nothing else to add so I just nodded slowly. Dad opened his mouth as though to comment but thought better and closed it again.

"Well, I'm so glad that we've all been introduced," Helena said brightly, taking a step back to put her arm around my dad.

Weird. Weird. Weird. A movie star just put her arm around my DAD.

Helena giggled, and I saw Marianne narrow her eyes at her in suspicion.

"I think it's time to tell them, Nick," Helena said enthusiastically, gazing up at my father, fluttering her eyelashes.

"Yes," he said deeply, taking her hand in his.

He took her hand. My DAD took the HAND of HELENA MONTAINE, a woman who happens to have a STAR on the Hollywood Walk of Fame. And she wasn't pulling it away. It was like it was a NORMAL THING TO DO.

On vacation in Portugal once my dad wore swimming trunks that had elephants sipping cocktails on them. And now he was holding Helena Montaine's hand.

NOTHING MADE SENSE ANYMORE.

He cleared his throat. "Marianne and Anna, we have something we'd like to tell you."

Marianne gave a fleeting nervous look in my direction.

Grinning like a mischievous teenager, my dad looked down at Helena, who turned to us excitedly with tears in her eyes.

"We wanted you both to know." She beamed. "We're getting married!"

"YOU LOOK *AWFUL!*"

Jess and Danny peered down at me where I was sitting in the corner of the hockey field.

"So what happened?! Why are we here? You hate sports!" Jess plonked herself down next to me.

"First of all, are you okay?" Danny asked, giving Jess an admonishing look. It's very difficult to hide your feelings from Danny, especially when he looks at you in such an earnest manner, which was what he was doing. Maybe it's something to do with those angelic curls, but whatever it is, it makes Danny seem very trustworthy.

"I'm fine." I sighed dramatically, picking at the grass.

Jess tutted impatiently, and I scowled at her for ruining the moment.

"We're here because every normal person—except for you, Jess—hates field hockey and would never hang out here voluntarily, and I don't want anyone else to overhear."

"Anna, what could be so bad? Did you step on a snail again?" She folded her arms.

"That snail came out of nowhere! And we promised to never speak of that day again."

"Well then, what's the problem?"

I took a deep breath and told them.

"Helena Montaine?! That's insane!" Jess gasped.

I nodded.

"Marianne Montaine was in your house?" Danny gaped.

"Yes."

"Wow." He looked dazed.

"Wipe the saliva off your chin there, Danny," Jess mocked before turning back to me and shaking her head in disbelief. "What did you do when they announced their engagement?"

Marianne and I had stood there in stunned silence. Helena and Dad glanced excitedly from one of us to the other, waiting for a positive reaction, but I had been unable to speak.

Marianne had eventually just blurted out, "Not again!"

"Now, Marianne," Helena said, raising her hand. "I know this is a shock, but that's unfair."

"Um, not really," Marianne snorted, looking at her

mom in disbelief. "How long have you known each other?"

"I can understand it's a lot to take in," Helena said hurriedly. "But we really do love each other."

"I have only said two words to Anna, if that—let alone to her dad!" Marianne looked exasperated. "Can't you be normal and let me get to know someone before you marry them? This is just like Rodney all over again."

Rodney Jenson, the man I assumed Marianne was referring to, was the second husband of Helena and a director. They had met while filming and married after dating for a year. It had ended after three months when he'd had an affair with the lead in his next film.

Or so the papers claimed anyway.

"It is not like that time," Helena said, suddenly very serious.

"Why are you always rushing into things?" Marianne demanded.

"I'm not always rushing into things," Helena said in a strained voice. "Neither Nick nor myself are spring chickens, darling. I've never felt this way before and, well, it just seems right."

Marianne let out a loud "Ha!" and swept her glossy hair over her shoulder in dismay. Dad and Helena both turned anxiously to me. I was trying to think of something appropriate to say or do other than running around the room waving my arms about and shouting, "WHAT THE . . . ? I'M SO CONFUSED! I JUST WANT TO HIDE UNDER MY BLANKETS FOR A MOMENT WHILE I WORK OUT WHAT ON EARTH IS GOING ON. I HATE EVERYONE."

Since that probably wasn't an option, and Marianne had already done the "beautifully glossy but ticked off" response, I decided to go down the sensible and mature route.

Despite the shock announcement, my burning chin was still a reminder of my earlier comment, and I wanted to give some impression of being a normal human being.

"Let's just all sit down and discuss this like grown-ups," I said eventually in a way I imagined someone sensible and mature might do, and took a step backward toward the sofa.

Unfortunately, I misjudged where the sofa was and instead backed into a side table. I stumbled and grabbed on to a lamp to regain my balance, but my foot got caught. As I fell backward, the lamp came down with me, causing a deafening crash.

"Let me get this straight," Danny interrupted at this point in the painful recollection. "You fell over. Onto your back. Flat out. In front of Helena and Marianne Montaine."

I nodded gravely.

"Then what happened?" Jess breathed, enraptured by the whole affair.

"It got worse," I sighed.

Helena and Dad rushed over to help me up. They both made a fuss, sitting me down in the big armchair and asking if my arm hurt. Marianne excused herself to get some fresh air outside. Just before she stalked out through the door, she gave me a look that I could only translate as disbelief. Disbelief, I imagine, that she and I would soon become members of the same family.

She stepped out of the front door while Dad went to make some tea and Helena sat on the sofa quietly next to me.

All I could do was stare at her in shock. Eventually she actually had to say, "Anna, are you all right? You're making me feel slightly uncomfortable."

I didn't want to say that I was all right, because I wasn't, but I also didn't want to make the famous actress sitting on my sofa feel uncomfortable. So I decided that instead of staring at her I would stare at the lamp that I had fallen over with. We sat in silence.

After an ice age, Dad came in with the tray of tea. Marianne also came back in and joined in with the silence that was encapsulating the room. Her hair was slightly more disheveled on her return, as though she had been running her hands through it a lot, and she looked irritated, glowering at her mother as she sat down. Helena must be used to it because she didn't flinch under her daughter's icy glare.

Unfortunately, Marianne hadn't shut our front door properly, so Dog must have managed to get out. Oblivious to Dog's adventure, Dad decided to attempt to make things a little better. He failed. "I think we'll all be very happy together."

Marianne and I stared at him.

"I'm really looking forward to us all getting to know each other." He beamed slightly manically.

Marianne and I continued to stare at him. My eyes were starting to hurt from all the staring.

Dad tried again. "I think it's going to be great!" he squeaked.

Helena nodded enthusiastically, looking at Marianne. "Of course it will!"

"It's madness," Marianne hissed at her.

This prompted a long silence once again. I was building up the courage to say something along the lines of congratulations just to lighten the atmosphere when Dog thought this would be an excellent opportunity to return from his solo venture and show off the fruits of his exploits.

Dog trotted into the living room carrying a live pigeon. Its wings flapped about his snout as he proudly presented it to Marianne.

When she looked up to see a Labrador with a pigeon in its mouth, Marianne screamed at the top of her lungs. Helena yelped and flung herself back against the sofa. Dad, in his infinite wisdom, leaped to his feet and commanded Dog to drop his offering.

Dog, for the first time in his life, actually did as he was told and dropped the gift. The pigeon immediately took flight, feathers spraying everywhere, and directed itself toward Marianne's head. She continued to scream and went to escape its line of flight, flinging herself off the sofa and onto the floor.

Helena lay flat on the sofa as the pigeon hysterically flew around the room, completely disorientated, attempting to escape the loud noise and commotion while Dad ran around, trying to chase it out of the door. In fact he was no help whatsoever and most likely made everything worse as the pigeon was now being chased by a madman flailing his arms wildly about the place. The pigeon went to the bathroom mid-flight, our sofas taking the brunt of the splatter. Marianne screamed in horror as her leather jacket became victim to a large dollop of white bird poo.

Dog further added to the commotion by joining Dad in running around the living room, barking the pigeon down. The excitement then got to be too much for Dog, and he began chasing his tail instead, still barking elatedly.

I dived behind the sofa at first, then crawled hastily toward the door, rolling clumsily into the hallway before shutting myself in the closet. It was just like a scene from *Die Hard*, except instead of Bruce Willis there was me, and instead of bullets there was pigeon poop.

Helena's voice rose above the shouts of my father before suddenly it went quiet. I pressed my ear to the door. The pigeon must have changed its position. There was movement in the hallway, around the vicinity of my closet.

WHAT IF THE PIGEON WAS OUTSIDE THE CLOSET?

I strained my ears for the sound of coos. Instead there was a rap on the door and an urgent voice said, "Anna?"

It was Helena. I concluded she was looking for help.

"Here, take this as a weapon!" I yelled dramatically, opening the door slightly and hurling the nozzle of a vacuum out into the hallway, slamming the door shut again.

"The pigeon is gone."

I clambered out. Dad shut Dog in the kitchen, and Helena

took a deep breath and announced that it might be best for her to go home.

Marianne was nowhere to be seen, but our front door was wide open, so I assumed she had stormed out soon after the pigeon had escaped.

Helena whispered something to my dad, said good-bye to me with a soft smile, and left.

"That is"—Danny searched for something positive to comment when I had finished relating the events to them—"quite an evening."

"And then did you talk to your dad when the others had left?" Jess asked, her eyes wide with disbelief.

"No, I went straight to bed. I told him I didn't want to speak to him."

"Did you talk to him this morning?" Danny asked, pushing the hair out of his eyes.

"No. Think I'm still in shock."

"Wow," Jess exhaled. "I wasn't expecting this."

"Me neither."

"Does this mean you're going to be famous? Like Marianne is?" Jess asked, her forehead creasing.

"No!" I exclaimed, my throat tightening.

"But you might get some attention," Danny reasoned, giving my knee an awkward pat. "We'll look after you though."

"Course." Jess nodded. "Maybe the best way to think of it is just, your dad is getting married. To someone who happens to act. And she's quite well known for acting. And her daughter is well known for going to parties. And they get photographed a lot." Jess looked like she'd confused herself with what she was saying and fell silent.

We sat there for a minute or so without speaking until the bell rang. Danny stood up and reached his hand out to help me up. "You know what I think?" he asked as he pulled me onto my feet. "I think this could be really cool."

"Huh?"

"Honestly, Anna, I don't think this is as bad as it seems. You've said before that you would have liked a sibling."

"Duh," I snorted. "But not a FAMOUS one who wears leather jackets. I always pictured myself with a sister who knows all the lines to all the same films so we could act out the best parts, and then one day we would create our own comic strip about two sisters who save London from destruction. You know, someone to eat Nutella out of the jar with while watching movies." I shrugged. "Normal sibling stuff."

Jess and Danny glanced at each other.

"You know what I mean," I sighed. "This is disastrous. Marianne and I could not be worse opposites. She probably hasn't even seen *Lord of the Rings*, let alone rehearsed the Mount Doom bit."

"Well, before you decide that this is the worst thing ever, let's just wait and see what happens. When are you seeing them next?" Danny asked.

"We're having dinner at Helena's this evening." I swallowed nervously. "That should be fun."

"Don't worry about a thing," Jess said, trying to sound jovial but failing badly. "I'm sure everything will be fine."

I don't know why everyone continues to lie to me in this fashion.

From: rebecca.blythe@bouncemail.co.uk

To: anna_huntley@zingmail.co.uk

Subject: Hello darling!

I know we spoke on the phone earlier today, which was lovely, but I just wanted to check that you're all right? You sounded a bit strained.

Are you still worried about setting that silly girl on fire? You're such a worrier. You get that from your father you know.

I never worried so much at your age. I remember when I was twelve I joined an interpretive dance crew. That's the sort of thing that would be perfect for you!

Love Mom xxxx

From: anna_huntley@zingmail.co.uk

To: rebecca.blythe@bouncemail.co.uk

Subject: Mom

Everything is fine. Really.

Interpretive dance? I'll pass, thank you. I'm already a big enough loser as it is. Interpretive dance would be a social death sentence.

Also you should know that I mentioned this to Dad and he said you've never joined an interpretive dance crew in your life. He says that you probably mean the time you toured Britain as a Morris dancer.

I hope that both of you know how much trauma is being embedded into my teenage years and thanks to my parents I'll no doubt end up in therapy until I'm in my late eighties.

So thanks for that.

Love, me xxx

I did think about adding a "PS Just so you know, Dad is engaged to Helena Montaine. Yeah, that really famous actress. Funny, isn't it!" in my e-mail, but then I thought I'd let Dad deal with that one. I'm sure Mom will be happy for him and everything, but putting her only daughter in that position without even warning Mom he is dating a public figure?

Yeah, Dad can face her wrath.

I had more pressing matters anyway. Here's a question I never thought I'd ask myself: What do I wear to go to dinner at a movie star's house?

"Anna," my dad was yelling across the landing, "we're going to be late! Just pick anything. Wear something casual. You want me to come help?"

I shut my door. Loudly.

After a lot of deliberating, I finally settled on black jeans and a pretty blouse that Mom had once bought for me in France in a bid to make me look more stylish. I looked at myself in the mirror and sighed. Why couldn't I look more like Marianne? Seriously, how come she always looks so good? Her hair is so thick and soft.

As I stared grumpily at my appearance, I could hear Dad getting frustrated outside my door, pacing around the landing and muttering to Dog about female time management.

"Lovely," Dad said hurriedly, hardly looking when I emerged. "Into the car. Now. It's rude to keep people waiting."

I ignored him in the car all the way there just to make sure he knows that I'm not going to make this whole process easy for him. Even if Danny was right and everything might turn out okay *and* Marianne could be the sister I've never had, there are more normal parent ways of introducing such a thing into your life, and I'm not going to let Dad get away with it just yet.

We turned into a gravel driveway, and a beautiful house loomed before us. I suddenly felt VERY nervous. Helena flung open the door and stood in the frame with her arms open and a huge smile on her face. "Welcome!" she cried as we shut the car doors and made our way over to her. "Anna, I'm so happy you're here."

She was wearing a very floaty orange dress with billowing sleeves so that when she stretched her arms out it looked kind of like she had wings. Like a bat or something. But a nice orange one.

She pulled me into a tight hug before embracing my dad with a big kiss on the lips. BLEUGH.

Why do adults think this is acceptable in front of their children?

Helena ushered us into the marble hall. It was huge and spacious, completely modern and exactly the sort of place you'd expect a movie star to live. Around the walls were framed posters of classic films, none of which featured Helena and several of which were signed by the stars or directors. There were two large potted plants on either side of the staircase that looked like mini palm trees, and the staircase itself had glass steps and white banisters.

It was the exact house I would envision for an actress like Helena Montaine. I gulped.

As Helena was fussing around, offering us drinks, Marianne came out from one of the side doors. She was wearing high-waisted jeans with a checkered shirt tucked in so her waist looked tiny and, even though she was in her house, she was still wearing big black heels and all these bracelets.

Oh God. Who looks like that when they're slobbing around their house?! Apparently It Girls do.

This was not a good start to the evening. I could never maintain a look like that around Dog. His hairs go everywhere, and he once ate a bracelet Mom brought me from Tanzania when I left it by accident on the coffee table.

"Hello," she said with a curt nod at both of us.

"Hi there, Marianne," my dad sang, trying too hard again.

"Hello," I replied, giving an awkward wave.

To be honest, there was no need for the awkward wave. I'm not sure why I made such a bizarre gesture. It certainly didn't lighten the atmosphere. Though it was better than "Howdy, partner," I guess.

Helena insisted on giving us a tour of the house after instructing a very reluctant-looking Marianne to prepare the drinks. She showed us the five bedrooms—two used, two spare, and one for when Helena was feeling "pensive" and wanted a different space. She let me poke around the huge en-suite bathrooms and the walk-in closets, admiring Marianne's extensive handbag and sunglasses collections.

"What's in there?" I asked, pointing at a door on the downstairs floor, once we had seen the kitchen, study, and living room.

"Oh, that's the screening room." Helena smiled.

"You have a screening room?" I asked, amazed.

"Duh." She grinned and pointed at herself. "Movie star."

"Anna *loves* films; don't you, Anna?" my dad said over-enthusiastically, clearly hoping this would change everything. "You can come over here and watch them on the big screen. Wouldn't that be *great*?"

I ignored him.

After the tour and some small talk about how school was going for me, and Dad's new yawn idea for a book he was working on, Helena invited us into the dining room for dinner. "I hope you're hungry," she said, excitedly leading us in.

Boy, had she made an effort. I've never seen so much sushi. The table was covered in large dishes and plates of fish and every kind of sushi you could think of: different combinations of maki and temaki rolls, edamame, spring rolls, teriyaki. We were about to consume the entire cast of *The Little Mermaid*.

Then I noticed the place settings. There were no knives and forks, just chopsticks. Let me tell you something about those of us in life who have very little coordination: chopsticks are EVIL.

"This is amazing, Helena," my dad said, beaming at her as he took his place. He looked at me expectantly.

"Yes," I said, trying to disguise my fear. "Amazing."

I tried to ignore what sounded suspiciously like a snort from where Marianne was sitting. Helena shot a glare across the table at her daughter.

These are the reasons why one should never eat sushi at a film star's house:

1. Chopsticks are HARD WORK. I felt exhausted about five minutes in from the trauma that came with each mouthful as I attempted to pick things up, dropped them, stabbed them, made

a mess, and then ended up using my fingers while spraying rice all over their shiny floor.
2. Every time you do drop a piece of sushi, while trying to carefully carry it to your plate from the platter using the dreaded chopsticks, your father will no doubt laugh too loudly and too nervously at you. If there are any It Girls that happen to be in the room, for example, Marianne Montaine, they will not laugh along with your deranged father but instead look at you gravely, as though they are slightly repulsed at you becoming one of their family but are too polite to show it.
3. You end up giving up attempting to eat because it is causing so much drama and thus return home starving and are reduced to eating Nutella out of the jar with a spoon.

"Why don't you two go upstairs and bond?" Helena suggested, clearly sympathetic to my disastrous sushi plight.

Marianne's face dropped, and I snorted wasabi sauce so hard I thought my head was going to explode.

"That's all right," Marianne said in a slight panic.

Normally I might be insulted by this but, still speechless from my wasabi brain-fire, I knew where Marianne was coming from. There had been no point in the evening that Marianne had been outwardly rude or uncivil. She had replied politely to my dad's eager attempts at conversation starters and had looked at me with genuine interest when Dad mentioned I had a school dance coming up.

Not that she had been particularly impressed with my response of, "Yeah, I don't have a date though. Might have to dance with a balloon again. Ha ha ha." In fact, she hadn't said anything at all.

It was just clear that Marianne Montaine and I had very little in common. The only thing that we shared was outrage toward our irresponsible single parents.

"I think that's a great idea." Dad nodded, looking at me. I knew he was trying to appeal to my forgiving side. I glared back at him.

"We can just . . . bond here," I suggested, giving Marianne a helping hand with the situation.

"I know!" Helena exclaimed, ignoring me completely. "Why don't you show Anna your shoe collection? Marianne has the most wonderful shoe collection!"

"Do I?" Marianne said in a strained voice.

"Anna would love that!" my dad announced.

"Would I?"

"Off you go, while Nick and I clear the table." Helena rose from her seat and picked up her dish.

Marianne, without looking at me, stood up slowly and made her way out of the dining room. I reluctantly followed, two pairs of eyes following me, our parents happily witnessing their plan come into action.

I stood awkwardly by Marianne's bed as she stepped into her walk-in closet. I told myself to try to keep an open mind about what kind of future stepsister relationship we might have.

"These are my pride and joy I guess," Marianne claimed, holding out a pair of black stilettos with the highest heel I have ever seen.

My open mind closed again. How could she walk in them and not trip? Some of us have trouble avoiding that embarrassment in flat shoes.

"They're . . . wonderful," I said. Silence reigned. "Um, do you . . . do you always wear heels on your feet?"

"Yes. Most of the time. And definitely on my feet." Marianne looked desperate and then went back to studying her shoe collection a little too intensely. I looked around the room for inspiration.

"Pretty cool that your mom's an actress," I began. "You must have seen loads of movies growing up."

"Not really." She shrugged, looking relieved that I had said something that another normal human being might come out with. "I didn't enjoy movies that much."

I blinked at her. She was reaching up for a handbag on her top shelf. "Wait a second." I couldn't help myself. "You don't enjoy watching movies?"

"Sometimes, I guess."

"I mean, your mom is in some classics," I said, still in shock by this discovery.

"Yes, I guess so." She nodded. "It's just not my thing."

"How come?"

"Well, my dad wasn't around. My mom was always away filming. If I stayed in and watched a film, I felt pretty lonely. And who wants that?"

"Um, yeah. *No one.*" I looked at the floor.

"Going out and talking to people, going to events and parties, made me feel less . . . ," Marianne said animatedly, warming up to what she clearly thought might be our first normal conversation and oblivious to the fact she'd just demoted me back to the ranks of complete loser. "Well, you know."

"Oh yeah," I said, not knowing anything about celebrity parties at all. "I *totally* know."

She looked at me in disbelief.

"Well, I know about the lonely bit anyway. Being an only child as well."

Marianne nodded. We sat in silence for a moment, both lost in thought.

"Well," I said eventually, relieved we'd found the tiniest sliver of common ground. "That was a nice moment."

"Um, right. So, this all seems a bit rushed. Your dad and my mom."

"Yes. I know. At least you don't have to get around the whole celebrity aspect. The whole you and Helena being these big famous stars. I mean it sounds weird, but I'm used to seeing you in magazines and reading about you in the papers. And now here you are in person and we're about to be . . . family."

Marianne grimaced slightly at the term "family" and then slumped back onto her bed. "I just hope it all works out." She let out a long, dramatic sigh.

I picked up a framed photo of Marianne with a group of beautiful girls, on a night out, hands on their hips, all posing perfectly for the photographer. I thought about the framed photograph on my desk of Dog wearing a cowboy hat. I put the photo down, a sinking feeling in my stomach. How could this possibly work out?

"So do I. Honestly though, I'm not sure any of it has really hit me yet." I picked nervously at the side of the table.

"Don't worry," Marianne replied calmly, staring at the ceiling. "It will."

And it did. Sooner than I was expecting.

10.

IT WAS DOG WHO GAVE ME AWAY.

We had been safely holed up in the closet, tucked behind the vacuum. I had been consoling myself for the last fifteen minutes, after the stormy events of the morning. Dad had been making an idiot of himself trying to reason with me through the door of my bedroom—completely unaware that I wasn't actually in it.

Serves him right. Thanks to him, I am a goner. Yes, thanks, Dad, for destroying my hope for a normal life.

If it wasn't for him and his frankly thoughtless engagement to a famous actress, then my Saturday morning would have been extremely pleasant. I would have gotten up, put on my bathrobe, greeted my previously faithful yellow Labrador, eaten bacon, and then spent the rest of the day enjoying my life.

Instead I got up, put on my bathrobe, greeted my traitorous

yellow Labrador, and went into the kitchen to find Dad standing in the corner, arms folded, hair disheveled, and looking like he'd just found Dog eating his *West Wing* box set.

"Whoa, Dad, too many whiskies last night?" I chuckled, grabbing the kitchen tongs and placing the bacon on my plate, careful not to wave it too near Dog's snout, which was cunningly resting on the side of the table. Dog was looking the other way though, trying to play innocent. He couldn't fool me.

Dad shook his head and cautiously pushed the newspaper on the table across to me.

On the front page was a picture of Helena at a recent premiere, and above it the headline read "Helena's engagement: third time lucky." It started with a nice introduction on her new engagement to "renowned journalist Nick Huntley," gave details about how they met and that, according to their source, the pair's current focus was "bringing the two families together."

But it didn't stop there. Oh no. The writer then went on to share a nice paragraph about Marianne and "Nick's preteen daughter, Anastasia," who were both "thrilled" about the engagement.

Thrilled? THRILLED? Who *was* this person?

I looked up at Dad. By the look on his face there was more. I read on with a very odd feeling in my tummy.

There was a smaller piece a few pages in, accompanied by a photo of ME strolling unaware down the road in my blouse and jeans with Dog trotting beside me yesterday evening after the dinner at Helena's. WITH SOY SAUCE SPILLED ALL DOWN ME.

Seriously. A little box in the corner of the article completely dedicated to me. The headline was "Britain's new It Girl?"

BY NANCY ROSE—THE DAILY POST

Now that Helena Montaine is getting hitched again, all eyes will be on Anastasia Huntley, Helena's almost-stepdaughter. While Marianne Montaine is no stranger to the spotlight, her new sister seems to opt for a more laid-back approach, choosing a simple—and casually "distressed"—outfit to take her dog for a walk in London. "Anastasia is new to fame and will most likely be shy," says our resident therapist. "One can only hope she will be a calming influence on Marianne. She must not get caught up in the fame game and lose sight of her goals." Marianne Montaine is well known on the party scene

> and has often been accused of setting a bad example for young girls. "Anastasia isn't like that," a source close to the family explains. "She's not into fashion, partying, or social events. But as she's so young, her father marrying someone so high profile has come as a shock to her. She is, however, taking it in stride."
>
> Could Ms. Huntley be a new kind of It Girl? We'll have to wait and see. . . .

An It Girl? *ME?!* I HAD SOY SAUCE ON MY TOP! And it was in a NATIONAL NEWSPAPER.

This was unimaginably awful. I guess I knew deep down that at some point it would be in the papers and it would be really embarrassing. But I didn't realize any focus would be on *me*. I thought my embarrassingly-in-love-for-his-very-old-age dad and Helena would get all the attention. I could never show my face at school again—I imagined how hard Sophie and Josie would be laughing right now at the thought that the biggest loser at school had been talked about in the papers in this way.

Why did it have to be sushi with soy sauce? WHY? Could have gone with a simple easy-to-eat dish like chicken, but no, it just HAD to be sushi with SOY SAUCE.

I will never eat soy sauce again. It is the worst of all the sauces.

"Dad, there's only one thing we can do. And I think you know what that is." I pushed the paper away and bit my thumbnail as he watched me carefully. "I'm thinking Italy. It's sunny there and there's a lot of cheese. That's all we need if we're talking basics."

"Anna." He sighed, looking exasperated, which if you ask me was very unfair of him. If anyone should have been looking exasperated, it should have been me. "What are you talking about?"

"Dad, we have to leave the country. And don't suggest Sweden. I know how you feel about those cinnamon buns, but we have to be logical here and Sweden can be very expensive."

"Anna, stop." Dad held up his hand. "We're not leaving the country. I know it's a lot to take in, but we're going to have to face it. They were going to find out at some point, and maybe it's better that it's out in the open. No more secrets."

"You expect me to stay in London? Are you CRAZY?"

He looked bewildered. "Why am I crazy to expect you to stay in London?"

"Dad, I'm not sure whether you're thinking straight right now. I know you had that limoncello at Helena's last night after coffee; I'm not sure if that's gone to your head. But surely you can appreciate that you have completely ruined my life."

"I think you're being a little dramatic now, Anastasia."

"And that's another thing. My full name, Dad, they used Anastasia! People at school are really going to go to town on that one."

"You have a lovely full name." He sighed. "I think you're overreacting slightly."

I glowered at him. "Dad! This is all your fault. Everyone in the world will read this and know that I am a massive loser who can't dress herself! This is the worst thing that has ever happened to me, and it's all because of you!"

I turned on my heel and walked straight out of there.

Then I walked back in to grab the bacon.

But THEN I walked out again, Dog in tow, and slammed the door, ignoring my dad's calls for me to come back to talk about it.

Talk about it! Ha! No way. I knew he would expect me to go shut myself away in the bedroom so I shrewdly shut myself away in the closet, taking Dog with me of course. It was a little annoying when Dog kept shoving his butt in my face as he got restless and decided to move around a bit, but eventually I managed to quiet him with half of my bacon and a tummy rub.

So I sat in the closet with my trusty sidekick, listening to Dad talk to no one through my bedroom door, and reflected on what this would mean.

I didn't even really know what being an It Girl meant. I just knew that Marianne was one. School was going to be one big nightmare. I could never leave the house again. Ever.

Either that or I could undergo some major plastic surgery.

Just as I was considering what facial features I could adapt, Dog greedily decided that he was bored of all the attention I was giving him, and he scrambled up, barged out of the closet, and went on the hunt for more bacon.

"Anna?" Dad said, as he heard Dog loudly bang the closet door open.

I felt so stressed and confused, especially now that Dog had deserted me and Dad was coming down the stairs hopefully feeling a little foolish, that I decided the best thing to do would be to get in the fetal position.

"Anna, what on earth are you doing on the floor? Are you in the fetal position again?"

"The fetal position is strangely calming. And you can't just stroll on in here, Dad! You have to knock."

"This is a closet. Not your bedroom. Why should I have to knock on my own closet doors?"

"Honestly, Dad." I sighed. "I shouldn't have to teach you these things. Go away."

"We have to talk," he insisted, leaning on the door.

"No we don't."

"Yes we do."

"Fine. I'm staying in here forever."

"Oh really?"

"Go away!"

"You're staying in the closet forever."

"You, of all people, shouldn't mock other people's life choices."

"Anna. You're lying down in the fetal position in a closet."

"I'm sorry, what exactly is your point here? YOU are marrying a ridiculously famous actress and RUINING my life."

"I am sorry about all this, Anna, really I am. They'll ignore you after a while. It's just the first flush of the news, and if you keep your head down and be boring, they'll leave you alone."

"Right, okay, thanks for the advice, Dad. You can go now."

He gave a big sigh, ran his hand through his hair, and then looked at me in silence for about a minute before obviously coming to the conclusion that his efforts would be fruitless.

He threw his hands up in the air, and started to shut the door again.

"Oh, and Dad," I said just before it was closed, "you better start looking for other schools in the area because there is no way I'm going back to mine after this. I think we should consider homeschooling."

"Anna, you are not getting out of school over this."

"You don't understand!" I cried, sitting up. "Dad, I'm not a popular student, okay? I'm a geek, a loser, whatever you want to call me. Bottom of the food chain. That article said that I'm an It Girl. Seriously, an *It Girl.* I am the LEAST It Girl–type person in my school. I never get invited to parties or do anything cool. Do you know how much people are going to mock me for this? They're probably all together now, laughing their heads off and drawing moustaches on my picture!"

"You're being ridiculous. Besides, I think you could be an It Girl if you wanted to. You could make the It Girl concept all about getting good grades and not going to cool parties but staying in to watch classic movies with your father."

Even my own father mocks me to my face. Why am I even on this planet?

"Dad," I said, taking a deep breath, standing up, and stalking past him toward the stairs. "I have decided to vacate the closet and will be hiding in my room. I ask you respectfully not to disturb me. I will either be writing what will most likely become a globally celebrated piece on the chilling and disturbing teenage years that you have subjected me to, or I will be brainstorming funding ideas so that I can escape to Bora Bora and spend the rest of my days tending to injured turtles or something else along those lines. Good day."

He muttered something under his breath as I ran up the stairs and jumped under my covers.

Hello! It's Anna here. Leave a message. Okay, bye!

BEEP

"Anna? It's your mom. I've been on the phone with your dad all morning, and he says you won't come and speak to him. Look, I know it seems awful now, but really, it's going to be okay, darling. Of course I'm going to kill your father on your behalf when I see him. There was once a series of pictures of me in the papers when I was accused of dating an elderly politician. It was, unfortunately, not true, but I got a flurry of freelance jobs from it. You see? It could be a blessing in disguise. Call me when you feel ready, always here for you. Lots of love, darling, bye."

Hello! It's Anna here. Leave a message. Okay, bye!

BEEP

"Anna, it's Jess. I've been trying to reach you all day. Look, it's not that bad, honest. They didn't even seem to notice—that much—that you'd spilled your dinner down yourself. Again. Come over, will you? Or let us come to you? Danny's got a brand new experiment that he wants to try out. Something to do with balloons and mayonnaise. Either way, it sounds entertaining. It will take your mind off things maybe. Call me!"

Hello! It's Anna here. Leave a message. Okay, bye!

BEEP

"Hey, Anna, Danny here. Hope you're all right. Anyway, I'm no good at voice mails. Never know what to say. Ha. Okay. Bye."

Hello! It's Anna here. Leave a message. Okay, bye!

BEEP

"Jess again. Okay, guilty—I tried to get Danny to call you to see if his calming tones might help lure you out of your solitude. Turns out he's useless at leaving messages. Seriously, save that one so we can tease him about it later in his life. Look, I know you're probably lying on your bed thinking about weird things like moving to Bora Bora or something random like that, but it might make you feel better to have some normal time with your friends. Here if you need us."

Hi, you have reached Nick Huntley's phone. Please leave your name, number, and any message, and I'll get back to you as soon as possible. Thank you.

BEEP

"Dad, it's me. I don't want to speak to you right now or come out of my room, so if you could just leave my lunch outside my door, that would be great. Thanks."

Hi, you have reached Nick Huntley's phone. Please leave your name, number, and any message, and I'll get back to you as soon as possible. Thank you.

BEEP

"Oh also, if you've made that pasta with that mascarpone sauce again, which, judging by the smell coming from the kitchen, you have, can you make sure you don't put any olives in mine? If you've already put them in, can you pick them out? And be thorough? Last time you left one in there and I ate it by accident and it was gross. Thanks, bye."

Hi, you have reached Nick Huntley's phone. Please leave your name, number, and any message, and I'll get back to you as soon as possible. Thank you.

BEEP

"You should know that I heard your reaction when you just listened to your voice mails, and I don't appreciate your tone of voice, even if you were talking to yourself. Stop knocking on my door; you'll break it—I've moved my dresser in front of it. And I think I pulled a muscle doing that, which is all your fault, because if you let me have a lock on my door I wouldn't have to go to such drastic measures. If you wish to communicate, you can leave me a voice mail as I do not wish to speak to you directly through any medium. That's why I keep hanging up whenever you pick up the phone. I would appreciate it if you let it go to voice mail for the time being.

Hello! It's Anna here. Leave a message. Okay, bye!

BEEP

"Anastasia Huntley, if you leave one more voice mail message on my phone, I will start getting extremely annoyed. I realize you're upset, but let's try to be mature about this. I'll leave you alone to have your space, and then you can come talk to me when you're ready. You're going to have to come out some time, and you're certainly going to have to come out when you go to school. I hope you're not going to be childish about that."

Hi, you have reached Nick Huntley's phone. Please leave your name, number, and any message, and I'll get back to you as soon as possible. Thank you.

BEEP

"I no longer wish to discuss this any further. Just leave the pasta and go. And, excuse me, I am not childish. I realize that I will, unfortunately, have to return to the lion pit that is school. Have some faith in your daughter. What do you expect me to do, purposefully injure myself or something so I can get out of going to school? Honestly, Dad, I'm not a baby."

OKAY, SO I PURPOSEFULLY TRIED TO INJURE MYSELF to get out of school. This is actually a lot more difficult than you would think. Plus I have a very low pain threshold.

It made sense that if I was mortally wounded I wouldn't have to go in on Monday and thus could avoid the torment of my peers awaiting me. On Sunday I tried rolling off the bed a few times in the hope of breaking an arm, but first of all, it hurt too much, and secondly, I guess the recurring thud of me falling to the floor made Dad concerned, as he came and banged on the door with his fist to find out what was going on.

"Nothing, Dad," I'd said innocently, after I had moved the dresser and opened the door to peek out at him. "But now that you're here, I actually wanted to ask you something. Where do we keep the hammer?"

This was an *obvious* joke, but he went crazy after that and then insisted on sitting in my room with his laptop working for the rest of the day so he could "keep an eye" on me. I tried to get rid of him by putting on some loud R & B and dancing around him in the hope he would give up and return to his study. Instead he typed away furiously and then suddenly yanked my speakers' plug out and threw the cable out of the window.

Dog didn't even get his walk on Sunday. He was so distressed by the missed opportunity to chase squirrels, his mortal nemeses, that he tried to climb into the washing machine in protest. Luckily, Dad pulled him out when he only had his head and front legs in there.

There had been a few photographers lurking outside our front door on Saturday and Sunday, but on Monday morning there were only a couple left. Helena's place, on the other hand, was apparently swarming with photographers. She too had decided the best thing to do was to lay low.

Marianne, however, had refused to let the public revelation of her mother's sudden engagement keep her from her social life. On Sunday there were several photos of her heading to a nightclub in central London posted online. In all of the pictures she was smiling broadly, looking very relaxed, and occasionally even giving a wave to the photographers. How does she do this? How can anyone seem so cool in this circumstance? And how can she look so good in a fedora?

After seeing the pictures I sneaked into my dad's room and tried on one of his fedoras, just to see if I should be donning something like that on Monday when I had to face the press. I did not look cool like Marianne. I looked like I was an extra in *Bugsy Malone*. I put the fedora back.

So the more determined members of the paparazzi still waiting outside our door weren't given anything particularly exciting on Monday morning, just boring me in my regulation school uniform and Dad with his arm protectively around my shoulders. I tried to block out their cries of "Anna! How do you feel about your dad's impending wedding?" and "Anna, are you going to be able to cope with your newfound celebrity?"

When we got to the front of the school building on Monday morning, Dad gave me this bizarre war-film-type "inspirational" talk about character building and how Huntleys always show strength in the face of adversity blah blah blah. I wasn't really listening. Instead I was staring at the school thinking of ways to get out of actually going in there. Dad was on to me though. He stayed by the car the whole time until I was in the building to make sure I didn't run in the opposite direction as soon as he'd turned the corner. Which of course had been plan B, after wounding myself.

Under his hawk-eye gaze, I slowly went up the school steps, my head down. I discovered that if I bent my head enough, my hair fell over my face. That way, people might not notice it was me; you know, I could be any old student.

This trick didn't quite go as planned as it was very difficult to see anything in front of me. As I went into the building, I tried to move as quickly as possible, roughly guessing the right direction to my locker. At first it worked perfectly—no one was looking in my direction as I made my way past the huddles.

But then I walked into a pillar.

My books went flying everywhere, and I landed unceremoniously on my butt. Everyone turned to look at the commotion, and immediately there was whispering, pointing, and, I believe, some snorts of laughter. I lay on the ground with my eyes shut, wishing I could sink into a black hole.

Eventually I sensed someone standing over me. *Please be Jess or Danny, please be Jess or Danny,* I pleaded in my head, my eyes still shut tight.

"You okay?"

It wasn't Jess or Danny. Please don't let it be who I thought it was.

I blinked up into Brendan Dakers's deep brown eyes. "Hey

there, Anna, you okay?" He stretched out his hand to help me up. I closed my eyes again.

"Anna?"

I opened one eye just to check and then shut it quickly. Yep, it was definitely Brendan Dakers. "Is everyone staring?"

"Um . . ." He hesitated. "Yes."

"Ah."

"It wasn't that bad."

"You're lying." I opened my eyes.

"No, really." He grinned. "I do that all the time. That pillar is a safety hazard."

"Can you tell people to stop staring? They'll listen to you."

Brendan smiled. "Come on, let me help you up."

I took his hand in a daze, and he pulled me to my feet. I was about to get out of his way and move on with my head down once more when he started talking to me again.

"Were you heading to your locker?"

"Um, yes. It's over there. You know, with all the . . . other lockers."

Seriously, WHAT IS WRONG WITH MY BRAIN?

"Right, cool. I'm walking that way too." He smiled and gestured for me to walk alongside him. This was my chance to say something funny and clever. Instead I walked beside Brendan Dakers with my mouth open. And everyone watching.

"Geez, people at this school are so unsubtle." He sighed, shaking his head at a particularly loud-whispering huddle of girls. They immediately went bright red and dispersed. "Ignore all of them," he warned.

As we reached my locker, he gave a salute. "See you later, Anna."

I stood in shock for at least two minutes, watching him walk away down the hall, before realizing that if I didn't stop staring I'd look like a bit of a stalker.

Brendan Dakers had spoken to me. ME! He had even been *nice* to me. The whole way through class that morning I sat dazed, reflecting on the morning's events. I decided that the reason for Brendan Dakers noticing and talking to me could be any of the following:

1. He mistook me for someone cool and popular. By the time he realized that I was actually one of the big nerds that he's not supposed to socialize with, it was too late and he had to see the conversation through to the end (unlikely because he found me on my butt).

2. He ate some bad shrimp or something and was sick and disorientated.
3. He took pity on the fact that I fell on my butt.
4. He likes Marianne–who does not fall on her butt–and wants me to introduce him to her.
5. He's just a nice person?
6. He believes that I actually am an It Girl.

Points 3 and 4 seemed the most likely. I asked Jess and Danny their opinion at lunch as we sat at our table, desperately trying to ignore the pointed looks of everyone around us.

"Maybe he was just being human." Danny shrugged, moving his vegetables around his plate. "People like Brendan Dakers do have the ability to be nice."

"But then why does he hang out with Sophie Parker and Josie Graham?" Jess asked, narrowing her eyes suspiciously at their table.

"He did stick up for me that time in class when Sophie was yelling at me about setting Josie on fire," I added.

"He said it was funny," Jess pointed out. "Not exactly backing you up. I don't know; it seems a bit odd to me that the day he decides to talk to you happens to be two days after your celebrity status appears in the papers."

"Or it just happens to be the day I walk into a pillar right in front of him. If it had been anyone else, he still would have helped them up, right?"

"Maybe." Jess shrugged. "It's not like Brendan Dakers has ever been horrible. He just chooses to spend his time with people who are. Maybe he thought you were someone else at first?"

"Yeah, I thought that." I nodded.

"I think you're both thinking about it way too much," Danny said, looking at us in exasperation. "Does it even matter?"

"Um . . . yes?" Jess and I chorused.

"It's not every day the most popular and best-looking boy in school talks to me, Danny." I sighed. "Normally I would be very happy right now. Sadly, my dad has ruined my life, so occurrences like Brendan Dakers talking to me are kind of overshadowed by the likelihood that everyone is going to be wetting their pants laughing at the fact that the papers suggested I might be the next newsworthy socialite. I bet Sophie and Josie are on their way to humiliate me right now."

"Um, first of all, Anna," Jess jumped in. "Just let Ms. Queen Bee and her evil minion try it. They'll have me to answer to."

"Yeah, me too!" Danny chimed in. "What?!" he asked, outraged at Jess's look of disbelieving pity.

I gave him what I hoped was a sympathetic and supportive smile.

"And *secondly*," Jess carried on, "it's not that bad. Being an It Girl could be very cool. *Couldn't it*, Danny?"

"Please don't call me an It Girl," I groaned, resting my forehead on my arms in front of me.

"It's, um, very cool," Danny mumbled through his lunch, looking at Jess perplexed. "Yeah, think of all the great things about it."

"Like what?" I muffled, not raising my head.

"Uh . . . ," Danny began, looking at the ceiling for inspiration.

"First, you're probably going to get lots of free stuff," Jess interrupted, poking Danny. "Celebrities always get free stuff. Clothes, shoes, accessories."

"You can say important stuff to the press!" Danny said desperately, scowling at Jess and rubbing his ribs. "You could speak out for those in need and bring attention to important charities."

"Like going to Africa and handing out rice?" I asked, lifting my head.

"Um. Sure?" Danny gave me an odd look. "I'm sure there's a charity out there that . . . goes to Africa and hands out rice."

"Danny," Jess said, sighing, "focus on the important things here. What about all the events she's going to get invited to. Premieres, black-tie galas, shop openings, fashion shows. That's the best thing about being a celebrity."

"Oh no," I whined, returning my head to my arms. "I'm going to have to learn how to walk like a normal person."

"Yes," I heard Danny say solemnly. "Yes, you are."

"Oh my God!" Jess suddenly gasped, reaching forward and shaking my arm so that I was forced to look up at her. "If you get tickets to On the Rox, you have to invite me. Marianne is definitely having a thing with the lead singer. I saw it online a couple of weeks ago."

"On the who?"

"On the Rox! They're my favorite band. Being Marianne's sister, you're bound to get free tickets."

"Stepsister," I corrected.

"Anna, who cares? Please, promise me you'll take me if you get tickets to see On the Rox. I would be the happiest person in the world."

"Promise." I smiled as she punched the air in victory. "I've never even heard of them, though."

"Of course you haven't! But you'll love them." Jess nodded vigorously with a huge grin. "Ask Marianne; she'll tell you all about them. It's so cool that she can date rock stars. You might start dating rock stars!"

I snorted. "Don't think so somehow."

"Well, if you keep snorting like that you certainly won't." Jess raised her eyebrows at me. "I bet you're going to meet some pretty amazing people. We're going to have to work on your conversation skills. You'll have to learn not to talk about Dog and Marvin comics so much in the presence of celebrities."

"Marvel. Not Marvin. Seriously, who is this Marvin person?"

Before Jess could answer, we were interrupted by two people suddenly standing by our table. I looked up to see Sophie and Josie smiling down at me. I immediately sat up straight. This was it. I braced myself for the onslaught of ridicule.

"Hey, Anna, sorry to disturb your lunch," Sophie began.

Jess was scowling so hard, I thought the waves of "go away" coming off her might knock Sophie and Josie off their far-too-high-for-school heels.

"I just wanted to say that we saw about your dad in the papers. That's really cool."

"It is?" I replied warily.

"Yeah, really cool. Anyway, my uncle remarried a few years ago, so I know what it's like to be in your position."

"Not quite the same thing," Jess muttered, picking up her fork and stabbing at a tomato.

Sophie ignored her. "If you ever wanted to talk about anything. Maybe fashion tips or . . . hairstyles." She eyed my head coolly. I was well aware that having been leaning on my folded arms for the majority of our lunch break I probably had a watch mark right in the middle of my forehead or something.

"Sophie has talked a lot with Brendan's mom about stuff like this," Josie said authoritatively. "So feel free to ask us any questions."

"How generous." Jess smiled sweetly up at them, like a viper would right before gobbling up a mouse.

"Um, yeah, thanks," I said, trying to elbow Jess.

"And listen, Anna." Josie took a deep breath. "The fire thing. It's forgotten. I know it was an accident. And you've clearly been under a lot of stress. It can't be easy being around people like Helena and Marianne when you're obviously not really . . . well, not that interested in their sort of things."

"Uh, right. Yeah. Thanks."

"Well, we'll catch up later," Sophie said, clearly blown away by how articulate and charismatic I was being now that

I was in the papers. And looking satisfied, they both waltzed out of the cafeteria.

"Wow." Danny shook his head and pulled his focus back to the vegetables.

"They are so weird." Jess laughed.

"Everyone is acting very strangely today. Maybe they all ate shrimp."

"Why are you talking about shrimp? You know I hate shrimp. Queen Bee and her sidekick are obviously interested in the new celebrity in their grade," Jess argued. "Maybe Sophie figures being nice to you can't hurt her chances of getting more attention."

"You think? I thought they were just being nice."

"I don't think so." Jess frowned. "What do you think, Danny?"

Danny finished off his water and slammed his glass down. "Girls are weird." He then began munching his vegetables.

"Thanks for that golden nugget, Daniel." Jess sighed. "You're as genius with advice as you are with voice mails."

"Honestly, Anna." Danny looked at me seriously. "I think you're going to have to prepare yourself for a lot of change."

Jess nodded slowly in agreement. I glanced around at the other students looking curiously at me. I gulped. I had a feeling Danny was, as always, right. There was a lot of change coming my way.

And I didn't have the first clue what to do about it.

TEN REASONS WHY BEING IN THE PAPERS IS NOT very fun:

1. Suddenly people look at you A LOT. This means that you have to try to not be yourself.
2. Because you are concentrating very hard on not being yourself, you do awkward things like walk into pillars and forget the entire English language when someone popular speaks to you.
3. You spend break times hiding in the prop closet of the drama department. This drawn-out solitary confinement leads to you slightly losing it and having a genuine conversation with a human-size sheaf of corn, last used in the school's production of *Joseph and the Amazing Technicolor Dreamcoat*.

4. People expect you not to do stupid things. You do stupid things regardless. They laugh at you.
5. There are photographers outside your school waiting for you to do stupid things.
6. In detention people won't stop asking you about the reason you're in the papers, making the detention teacher Mr. Kenton get very angry at no one being quiet.
7. The detention teacher ends up spilling his coffee over his white shirt midway through shouting, giving you an evil glare as though it is all your fault.
8. At the end of detention someone actually asks for your autograph so that they can sell it on eBay.
9. When you say no, they call you a "grouch."
10. You will most likely lose the only two friends you have due to the odd things you start to do that will freak them out, like having conversations with a sheaf of corn prop. You will therefore be left with very little dignity and a yellow Labrador that will betray you for bacon.

I never thought I'd be grateful for detention, but it was nice to put off going home back to my dysfunctional family life for another hour. Sure, it was very annoying when people like Joe Winton in the grade above kept asking for Marianne Montaine's number—yeah, Joe, because a famous It Girl is going to want to date a thirteen-year-old who is currently in detention for disrupting assembly by pulling down a fellow student's pants—and I could have done without all the questions about why, now that I'm a celebrity, no one has "fixed" my hair yet.

But once everyone shut up, it was nice to get some work done. Not that Connor let me get away with it completely that first detention after it had been in the papers.

"It's funny," he'd said, leaning back in his chair, chewing a pen. "I don't remember seeing 'Become Britain's new It Girl' on your list of ambitions. . . ."

"It wasn't on the top of my list, no." I sighed, slumping into my chair next to him.

"Hey, *Anastasia*."

I knew that would come back to haunt me.

Max was a friend of Connor's who made frequent detention appearances too. "Yes, *Maximillian*?"

"If you ever need anyone to come with you to any of those

celebrity parties where there are going to be supermodels and famous actresses looking for a fella to show them a good time, then I'm your man." He winked at me.

"Wow, Max, thanks. That's a pretty irresistible offer."

Connor snorted.

"Well, that's what the ladies tell me." Max grinned.

"His mom," Connor interjected under his breath. And for the first time since the newspaper article, I laughed out loud.

"That's what I was looking for, Spidey. Nice to see you smile today." He slid his sketchbook across to me. "Now, on to more important things. What do you think of this new character I've been working on? I'm not sure if he looks too obvious. You think I should tone down the muscles?"

It was my Mr. Kenton–supervised hour sanctuary of normalness. And it soon became my favorite part of the whole day.

Outside of detention everything was going wrong. Not only was school a catalog of embarrassing un–It Girl displays from me, Dad was paranoid about me leaving the house without him in case I got pounced on by rogue members of the press. It was getting out of hand. I was starting to feel like Frodo in *Lord of the Rings* when Sam wouldn't leave him alone. Except instead of being on a mission to return a ring, I was on a mission to keep my two remaining friends who in school saw me being ritually laughed at and outside of school didn't see me at all. And instead of an optimistic hobbit, who handily happened to be an excellent chef, following me around, I had a grumpy old man who insisted on saying things like "what is the world coming to" every five seconds and kept putting olives in pasta sauce.

Something had to be done.

It was a Wednesday afternoon, school had finished early—there was no detention that day, as Mr. Kenton had been struck down by the flu and no one could cover for him at such late notice. The sun was out, Dog was restless and, despite not having my usual refuge of detention, I was in a relatively good mood.

Jess and Danny were both busy, so I went home and decided to take advantage of the cloudless sky and take Dog for a walk. I picked up Dog's tennis ball and leash, and immediately Dad was standing in the doorway looking suspicious.

How come parents always know when you're thinking of doing something you shouldn't?

"Are we going on a walk?" he asked nonchalantly.

"Dog and I are going on a walk," I said firmly. "Once he stops running around the house."

Dog, having seen his mangled old tennis ball in my hand, had instantly sped off to do some laps of his territory in joy.

"I'm coming with you."

"No, Dad, you're not. You're smothering me." I sighed. "I don't want to have to start hiding your tea just to have some alone time."

Dad gave me a funny look.

"I wouldn't underestimate me," I stated matter-of-factly, shoving a set of keys in my pocket.

"What about the paparazzi? You know they might be out there."

"There are none out there. I checked through the window. I think they've gotten bored of the same photos of me going to school and coming back from school. Even the most imaginative journalists can't do much with those."

"I don't like you going on your own," Dad huffed.

"I won't be long. I'll just go to the park. I'll take my phone. Dog will be with me. I can always set him on some press members. I'll tell him they're squirrels in disguise."

Dad let out a long, tired sigh. "Fine. But I want you to take something with you just in case." He ran upstairs.

"Like what?" I called up after him. "I hope you're not expecting me to carry around your old baseball bat that's autographed by that dude no one has heard of?"

While Dad was rummaging around upstairs, I managed to tackle Dog midway through one of his circuits. I got the leash around him and then instructed him to sit. He decided instead to headbutt the telephone table. I left him to it.

Dad came trundling down the stairs holding what looked like a mini hollow wooden log. "Here," he said, holding it out to me. "It's a duck call from my hunting days. Just in case."

"Just in case of *what*?" I asked in utter amazement, looking at my father who had clearly lost his mind. "A duck has an emergency and needs to gather its far-flown family?"

"Don't joke, Anna. Put that in your pocket, and it could come in handy to whack someone in the head with. Self-defense."

"Dad. I mean this with kindness. I think you need to sit down and consider your state of mental health. You can't expect me to use a duck call as an assault weapon. I'm going to go now." I put the duck call in my pocket just to make him happy and then led Dog out of the house—or, rather, Dog enthusiastically pulled me out of the house—looking back to see my dad peering through the curtains.

Honestly, with a dad like mine, how can anyone expect me to be normal?

I hadn't been at the park long when I heard someone call my name. I turned around expecting to see one of the paparazzi who clearly hadn't got the "I'm boring" memo, but instead saw Brendan Dakers making his way toward me, wearing soccer gear and looking perfect as usual.

"Hey," he said, jogging up to me and pushing the hair out of his eyes. "I thought it was you standing there."

"Oh. Yeah. It's me. Standing here. Just with my dog."

GOOD ONE, ANNA. Please, God, let me become better at talking to boys before I hit old age, otherwise I'm going to be on my own for eternity.

"Yeah, I can see." He smiled at Dog. "How's things? Haven't had a chance to talk to you at school."

"Everything's okay. My dad is being weird, but that's about it."

"Yeah, my dad was weird when he remarried." Brendan rolled his eyes. "Kept trying to act half his age. It was bad."

"Yeah."

The conversation came to a bit of a standstill as I struggled for something interesting to say, and I imagine Brendan struggled to work out a way of getting out of talking to me for much longer.

"Your dog know any good tricks?" Brendan eventually

asked, looking at Dog, who was sitting perfectly still, staring at the ball in my hand. Just as he had been doing the whole time we'd been talking.

"Pretty much just fetch. You want to throw it for him?" I asked.

Brendan looked at the mangled, slobbery tennis ball I was holding out to him and didn't look all that enthused, but he took it anyway. Then, with much more power than I could ever hope to achieve, he hurled it into the stretch of trees and bushes nearby. Dog zoomed off in pursuit, diving headfirst into the overgrowth.

"Wow!" I exclaimed. "Impressive throw."

"Maybe it was a bit far. Will he make his way back?" Brendan asked, looking concerned.

"Who, Dog? Please. He has incredible navigation. And fetch is pretty much his only talent. He'll be back before you know it," I assured him confidently.

Five minutes later, we were still standing quietly awaiting the return of Dog. I was getting a little anxious but didn't want to show it. Brendan was fidgeting next to me. I don't know why I couldn't think of anything to say. Normally with Jess and Danny the conversation flows freely. But with them I don't have to try to say something impressive. I was very aware that Brendan was regretting being polite and coming to talk to me in the first place, which didn't put me more at ease.

"He'll be back soon," I said for maybe the tenth time. We continued to stand there in silence. I put my hand in my pocket and felt the duck call.

"This could work!" I said, pulling it out.

"What on earth is that?"

"You blow into it, and it makes a duck sound. A quack. You use it to make ducks come to you."

I decided to give him a demonstration, making a couple of loud quacks until Brendan held up his hand. I stopped.

"Why do you even have that on you?"

"Uh, as a self-defense weapon."

Brendan stared at me.

"Basically . . ."

But just as I was going to launch into a gabbled explanation about my crazy father and the duck call, we heard a rustle from the area where Dog had disappeared. Brendan looked at me hopefully. Dog victoriously emerged from the bushes and headed in our direction. I would have rejoiced, but it was difficult to once I realized what my Labrador was holding.

Dog was carrying a picnic basket.

Brendan and I looked at each other. "I don't think that's what I threw," Brendan said, confused.

Before I could answer, a man also emerged from the trees,

his face bright red with anger and in pursuit of Dog, who was ignoring this stranger's calls for him to stop. Instead, Dog neatly dropped the basket at my feet.

"Your dog has ruined my picnic!" the man cried in outrage.

"I'm so sorry!" I began to bend down to pick up the basket and return it to him. I couldn't even look in Brendan's direction. This was mortifying.

But Dog was not going to give up that easily. Not when he had gone to so much effort to get his prize. Upset at the lack of enthusiasm for his presentation and, no doubt, taking it upon himself to punish me, Dog lifted up his back leg and proceeded to pee down the side of the basket.

I covered my mouth in horror, Brendan took a step back, and the owner of the picnic basket stopped in his tracks as we all watched Dog finish his business and look extremely pleased with himself.

Why me?

From: jess.delby@zingmail.co.uk

To: anna_huntley@zingmail.co.uk

Subject: Not that bad

I'm sure Brendan found it funny?

J x

From: anna_huntley@zingmail.co.uk
To: jess.delby@zingmail.co.uk
Subject: Re: Not that bad

No.

Love, me xxx

From: jess.delby@zingmail.co.uk
To: anna_huntley@zingmail.co.uk
Subject: Re: Not that bad

Well, then he must have no sense of humor. It sounds hilarious.

J x

From: anna_huntley@zingmail.co.uk
To: jess.delby@zingmail.co.uk
Subject: Ha ha

Hilarious is not how I would describe the incident. It's definitely not how Dad would describe it either. Turns out the basket was from Fortnum & Mason. You can imagine that it's not a very cheap bill to have to pay. Brendan is going to tell everyone, isn't he, and then they're all going to make fun of me.

Even more than usual. What happens if the newspapers find out about this?? The basket man could sell his story!

I'm doomed.

Love, me xxx

From: jess.delby@zingmail.co.uk

To: anna_huntley@zingmail.co.uk

Subject: Re: Ha ha

You don't need to worry, you're an It Girl these days, remember? People won't be making fun of you.

Although Dog may have ruined your chances of Brendan Dakers realizing you're his one true love.

The newspapers won't care about a dog peeing on a basket. They'll be too busy reporting on real stuff like war zones and which celebrity baby dresses better.

J x

From: anna_huntley@zingmail.co.uk

To: jess.delby@zingmail.co.uk

Subject: Re: Ha ha

I hope you're right. Otherwise you and Danny will have to face up to being friends with the biggest embarrassment of all time.
I haven't even told you the part about the quacking.
Maybe I could try to talk to Brendan? And ask him not to tell anyone? Then I wouldn't have to worry about the newspapers or people like Sophie and Josie finding out!
I've got to speak to Brendan before school. I could try to win him over. I could offer him the chance to meet Marianne in exchange? Then he might consider keeping the whole thing to himself. Plus he might like me more if he gets to meet Marianne, right?
I'm sure Marianne wouldn't mind. The other day she gave Dog a pat on the head. Definitely a good sign I think.
Love, me xxx

From: jess.delby@zingmail.co.uk
To: anna_huntley@zingmail.co.uk
Subject: Calm down

Huh?

Look, I don't think Brendan telling people would be that much of a problem. Who cares what Sophie, Josie, or anyone at school thinks?

Secondly, you don't have to worry about me and Danny, Anna. We're not going to be fazed by something like your dog peeing on a basket.

What do you mean by "the part about the quacking"?

J x

From: anna_huntley@zingmail.co.uk
To: jess.delby@zingmail.co.uk
Subject: Re: Calm down

Um . . . nothing. Forget I said anything.

Love, me xxx

From: jess.delby@zingmail.co.uk
To: anna_huntley@zingmail.co.uk
Subject: Re: Calm down

What do you mean by the part about QUACKING?!

J x

From: anna_huntley@zingmail.co.uk

To: jess.delby@zingmail.co.uk

Subject: NOTHING

It's not very interesting.

Just, you know. I may have made quacking sounds using a duck call in front of Brendan.

That's all.

Love, me xxx

From: jess.delby@zingmail.co.uk

To: anna_huntley@zingmail.co.uk

Subject: (no subject)

There are no words.

J x

From: anna_huntley@zingmail.co.uk

To: jess.delby@zingmail.co.uk

Subject: Re: (no subject)

I hate my life.

Love, me xxx

13.

I COULDN'T BE SURE IF BRENDAN HAD TOLD ANYone about the basket day. I kept waiting for someone at school to make a snide comment about it, and I was absolutely certain it was going to appear at some point in the tabloids. I could just imagine it:

"IT GIRL'S DISORDERLY DOG PEES ON PICNIC"

But a few days later and there hadn't been a word of it in the papers. Perhaps the basket man hadn't realized who I was. Or perhaps the bigger basket plus large bottle of champagne sent to him from my father had done the trick. Either way, it looked like I was safe from national shame.

I was more worried about school. Earlier this year they would have been like, "Anastasia who? Isn't that a dead Russian princess? I don't think she goes to school here. Oh! The girl who set someone on fire . . . right." But now, thanks to Dad's impending marriage to the most famous actress in the whole world, the humiliation would be tenfold. I would have to be homeschooled. I would spend most of my days crying, remembering the two precious friends I used to have. And no one would be there to comfort me. Apart from Dog. Who really, if we think about it, would be the reason I no longer had any friends in the first place.

And so, I waited for someone to make fun of me at school, for the whispering and laughing to begin, or for everyone to completely ignore me.

But it didn't happen.

What did happen was very strange. No one said anything at all about it the entire week. Not even Brendan. Everyone was completely normal. I mean, he said hi to me when we passed in the hall, but not once did he ask me to stay at least five feet away from him or anything.

"What did you expect?" Jess laughed as I related how confused I was. "For Brendan to tell everyone that your dog peed on a basket in front of him and for no one to want to be friends with you anymore?"

Well. Yeah.

"It's not a big deal." Jess shrugged, digging in her bag. "It's not like you set someone on fire. HA."

Even more strange was Sophie cornering me by the water

fountain at the end of the week. I wasn't particularly happy about this because I find water fountains very stressful, especially if the arc of water isn't pronounced enough. Sometimes it's a dribble, and you have to shove your head right down and purse your lips out weirdly like a fish. That was exactly what I was doing when the most popular girl in the grade decided to speak to me.

I was so surprised when I raised my head to see her standing right there that I dribbled a little water on myself. She witnessed this and paused as though thinking carefully about whether or not talking to me was worth it.

"Hey, Anna," she said brightly once I'd wiped myself down. "Why don't you sit with us at lunch today?"

I looked around me just in case there was another Anna in the line behind me. I didn't want another "awkward wave on the volleyball court" situation. "Me?"

"Yes." She laughed. "Would be nice to catch up."

I thought this was an odd thing to say considering Sophie and I have never really talked before, so "catching up" would mean catching up on our entire lives starting with the day of birth.

"Brendan told us that he saw you last week in the park with your dog," she continued. I immediately tensed, ready for an onslaught of mockery. "You have a Labrador right? I love dogs. I'd like to meet him. Brendan said he was cute."

I looked at her in confusion. "Oh. Yeah, well, he's great. You can definitely meet him."

"Nice. Well, see you at lunch then." She flicked her hair, twirled around, and sauntered back down the hall, her short skirt swishing from side to side in time to the clips of her shoes.

I couldn't work it out for a while, but then it hit me midway through French. Not only had Brendan been kind enough not to tell them what had gone down at the park, the mere fact that he had mentioned hanging out with me had prompted Sophie Parker to want to hang out with me.

This was a cause for note-passing with Jess.

Guess what?

I hate this game.

What game?

The Guess What game.

How can you hate the Guess What game?

Because it's annoying. Just tell me what you want to say.

It's technically not a game. It's more of a lead-up to a revelation.

But why not just lead with the revelation?

You're taking the fun out of guessing.

FINE. Start again.

Guess what?

I don't know, Anna. What?

Sophie Parker wants us to sit with her at lunch!

She what? That's so weird! Did she talk to you?

By the water fountain.

You must have hated that. Did you dribble? You

always dribble afterward. You need to remember to close your mouth on that last sip.

I did not dribble.

I can tell you're lying. But tell me more about what happened.

She said that Brendan told her about hanging out with me at the park and he thought Dog was cute. And she said we should sit with them at lunch.

Wow, that's odd. Do you think we HAVE to sit with them?

It would be a bit rude not to. She purposefully found me to ask us to sit with them at lunch. Don't you think we should?

I think it's weird to formally ask someone at school to sit with them at lunch. Like she's royalty or something and she's granting permission.

She is sort of school royalty, wouldn't you say?

No, I would not say Sophie Parker is school royalty. Although she probably likes to think she is. I guess we can sit with them though—there are SOME nice people in that group. And I guess as it's Friday we can throw caution to the wind.

YAY!

What have I told you about playing it cool?

Sorry. Yeah, sure, whatever, we'll sit with them, whatever. That's cool, yeah.

You'll get there one day. Keep practicing.

Everyone in the cafeteria was looking at us at lunch break. It's something I suppose people like Brendan get used to, being so popular and good-looking. I put my tray nervously down next to Sophie's, and Jess and Danny put theirs opposite. James Tyndale was in the middle of a story when we joined them. Brendan gave me a smile as I sat down, making me blush, and then he returned his attention to James.

"That was the funny thing though. It wasn't like I had ever

been there before. Completely coincidental that—"

"Anna, what's Marianne Montaine like?" Josie loudly interrupted right in the middle of his sentence.

Everyone at our table turned to look at me.

"Uh, yeah, she's nice. I haven't seen her lots, but she seems cool." I tried to keep it vague, hoping no one would probe into the details of mine and Marianne's lack of similarities.

"Do you think you'll get to go on film sets with Helena?" Sophie asked eagerly.

"I don't know, maybe. I hope so. It'd definitely be cool to see what happens behind the scenes."

"Yeah, that would be cool," Brendan agreed, playing with a ball in his hand. "You must get to go to some exclusive events."

"Are you going to go to all her premieres?" Josie gasped excitedly. "I am so jealous. You'll probably meet loads of famous people. You HAVE to date someone from a boy band."

"Why does she have to date someone from a boy band?" Brendan asked, rolling his eyes.

"Because," Josie said, with an air of authority, "that's what It Girls do."

"I'm not an It Girl," I said quickly. "I don't know why the

papers keep saying that. It's only because of Marianne. I haven't done anything differently."

"Except for have lots of dinners with a hugely famous actress who is about to become your stepmother." Jess smiled.

"Yeah." I grinned back. "Apart from that."

"I don't think you should date someone from a boy band," Brendan stated, looking at me.

There was a pause, and then Sophie laughed stiffly. "What does it have to do with you, Brendan? You can't tell her what to do."

"That's just not you, Anna," he said, looking at me intently before turning back to the boys at the other end of the table. "James, finish that story you were telling us earlier. I wanted to hear the end."

Danny raised his eyebrows at me as I sat there with my mouth open, ignoring the heat rising to my cheeks. What had just happened? I decided I wasn't going to think too much about Brendan's comment. Nope, not at all.

Obviously this was impossible, and I thought about it every second of the rest of the day.

Even in detention I was distracted. "You thinking about your new friends there, Spidey?" Connor said suddenly, waking me from my daydream about Brendan Dakers taking me to a premiere.

"What?"

"That's the first time I've said something controversial about Spider-Man and you haven't reacted. I was wondering if your expanding social circle had something to do with your short attention span today. What was the conversation like at lunch? I've always wanted to know what that group talks about."

"I didn't see you in the cafeteria. Where were you sitting?"

"I'm not surprised you didn't see me. You seemed pretty focused on your own table."

"They're nice." I shrugged, sensing that Connor was waiting for an opportunity to make fun of something. "You should have come and sat with us."

Connor went "HA!" and I scowled at him. He did have a point though—it was a stupid thing to suggest. The student population had already been thrown by the fact that Jess, Danny, and *I* had been sitting with Brendan and Queen Bee. If Connor had sat down with us, the school would have been thrown into a frenzy.

"I would be wary of that crowd if I were you," he said irritatingly, turning a page in his sketchbook. "Brendan, Sophie, and those guys who think they're too good for everyone else. They're not all that."

"Thank you for your opinion," I replied curtly.

"I'm just saying, Anna, you're smart. They won't get that."

I looked up. He didn't call me Anna very much these days.

"I'll have you know that Brendan said something along those lines to me this exact day."

"Did he really?" Connor chuckled. "Well, I hope he means it."

How rude. I frowned at him and returned to highlighting my chemistry notes. I don't know why his comments bugged me so much. Connor Lawrence is hardly an expert on these sorts of things. And it's not like he's even talked to those guys before, so he doesn't know what they are like.

Still, I felt angry at him. The fact that I was actually starting to make new friends at school could only be a good thing. For the first time maybe ever, I was being noticed by people who were popular and fun, and it felt good. I wasn't going to let people like Connor Lawrence, who have no idea what they are talking about, ruin it for me.

Hello! It's Anna here. Leave a message. Okay, bye!

BEEP

"Hi, Anna. It's Sophie, from school. I know you probably have a lot going on this weekend, but if you're free, you should come join us at the park on Saturday. Everyone will be there. Would be nice to hang out more. And you can bring your dog maybe. Have a nice evening! Bye!"

14.

MARIANNE LOOKED AT ME WITH AN EXPRESSION of confusion. "What did you just say?"

I sighed and put my glass of seltzer down. "How do you make a boy like you?" I repeated slowly. Marianne blinked at me, and Helena chuckled. My dad leaned back in his chair with his eyebrows raised—but I resolutely ignored him. I don't know why they all looked so surprised. It is a perfectly valid question to ask a glamorous celebrity icon.

We were at Helena's favorite glitzy London restaurant. I wasn't that enthusiastic about the idea of another dinner with them; that's all we seemed to have done so far: dinners. I was starting to run out of conversation with Marianne. There are only so many times that you can comment on your meal. I couldn't think of any more adjectives these days. "Wow, this is delicious!" "Mine is scrumptious!" "Is yours as mouthwatering as mine?" "This is fantastic." "These ingredients are just so fresh!"

I suggested to Dad that we all do an activity together like Laser Quest or something. You can really get to know a person through Laser Quest. But Dad just chewed on the pen he was holding and went, "It's still early, Anna. I'm not sure we're ready for Laser Quest."

So there we were having another expensive and slightly awkward dinner. It wasn't all bad though—my steak and French fries were awesome. Dog would have been beside himself with jealousy. A bit like I suspect Marianne actually was as she sat and nursed a salad. Not wanting her to be distracted by my superior food choices, I tried again, reaching for a French fry and dipping it in some ketchup. "Seriously, I need to know. I'm twelve and I don't have a clue. Plus I'm not asking Dad."

"Hey, why not?" Dad protested. "I'd be a great help. You've just never asked."

"Oh really? Go on then—how do you get boys to like you?" I asked, humoring him.

"Cook them a steak," he announced proudly, pointing at my dish.

"Cook them a steak?" I sighed. "Dad, you expect me to

stroll on into school and offer the most popular boy in class a steak? He already thinks I'm a loser. I don't want to look completely crazy."

"He's the most popular boy in class?" Marianne asked quietly, her interest sparked.

"Yeah." I picked up my steak knife. "I know. He's never going to notice me. But I wondered if you might have any tips. You and Helena seem like the best people to ask."

"Well"—Helena smiled and placed a hand on her heart—"I am flattered, I have to say. Anna, I have several tips when it comes to winning the heart of the object of your affections. Would you like me to run through them?"

"I would very much." I nodded, digging into my perfectly cooked steak.

Marianne let out a long sigh. "Here we go," she said under her breath as her mom launched into a monologue on the art of male attracting. I wasn't sure, but I think Marianne might have caught my eye and given me a very slight, barely there glimpse of a smile.

It counts.

HELENA MONTAINE'S TIPS ON HOW TO MAKE A BOY LIKE YOU

1. First, one must look fabulous. Boys do not like girls who fall out of bed and decide that will do. That will most certainly NOT do.
2. Hair–must be always washed. The non-washed-hair look is for try-hards, and they are always a bore.
3. Nails–chipped? Absolutely not. Boys will not want to kiss a girl who can't stay on top of her hand maintenance. A quick coat of color, top-coat, and voila! The boy is yours.
4. Clothes–an expression of your personality, so wear what you wish. However, holes, scuffs, or rips, unless they are purposefully ripped by a designer, are unacceptable. Throw the item away.
5. Now that you're looking fabulous, it's time to focus on what you say–draw them in with your wit and charm.
6. If you don't have wit and charm, draw them in with your eyes. Eye contact is vital. Don't scare them of course.
7. Compliment them ALL THE TIME. I like to accentuate how masculine they are. For

example, insist on him opening the stuck window or the tough jar lid and then, when he is victorious, look at him in awe and tell him how strong he is.

8. Act like you are good at everything without being boastful–in fact you are incredibly modest about being good at everything. If possible, get your friends to comment on your array of talents while you blush and say, "She's exaggerating." But we all know she's not.

9. Laugh–keep it dainty and feminine. A hearty laugh is for farmers.

10. Anecdotes–humor is essential, but never be the butt of a joke.

11. Until there is a ring involved, you should not eat indelicate food in front of him such as a burrito or hamburger. Remember, you are an elegant female, superior to him in every way.

"What happens if you've set someone on fire and your dog has peed on a picnic basket in front of him?" I asked when Helena was finished. "Hypothetically."

"If he really likes you, things like that won't matter," Dad said encouragingly. "Who is this boy you like?"

"Gross, Dad. I'm not talking about this with you."

Dad looked offended. "Why not?"

"Because you're my dad. And that's weird."

"Marianne, you must have some advice for Anna? You've constantly got boys after you." Helena smiled at her daughter, who was picking cautiously at her salad.

"Mom, that's not true." Marianne rolled her eyes.

"It is. She's being modest. Who's that boy in that band who's crazy about you? The one in that band that makes the loud music. You know, In the Rox, isn't it?"

"ON the Rox! And, no, he is not crazy about me." Marianne blushed.

"I've heard of that band," I said, sitting up straight. "My best friend, Jess, she loves them."

Marianne nodded. "Yeah, they're good." Her phone beeped. She bent down to her handbag and started reading her texts.

"Well, aren't you going to tell Anna how you caught his eye?" Helena frowned while Marianne typed away at her phone.

"You don't have to," I said as Marianne shot her mother a

warning look. "It was a stupid question. And pointless anyway. No boys notice me. And this one definitely won't. Plus, he likes the most popular girl in the school, which makes sense. She's very beautiful."

"Nonsense," Helena stated firmly. "I'm sure you've got hundreds of better qualities than she has."

"No, really, I don't." I sighed. "It's like she's a beautiful, graceful swan, and I'm a clumsy newt."

"Don't worry, darling," my dad said, leaning over and giving my hand a comforting pat. "I've always been very fond of newts. I remember finding one in a pond as a boy. I named him Harold."

Comforting.

From: marianne@montaines.co.uk
To: anna_huntley@zingmail.co.uk
Subject: Hi

Hey, Anna,

Hope you don't mind me e-mailing.

I've been thinking about dinner. Sorry if I seemed rude when you asked for my advice on boys. It was a bit weird talking about it in front of our parents, don't you think . . . ? Anyway I thought I would e-mail you about it instead. I've always found that if I feel good, then I'm more relaxed and confident, which boys like. So if you feel pretty, that will come across. And don't worry about him being popular and you feeling like you're not. If he's nice, then none of that will matter. He'll notice you either way.

Anyway better go. I'm in the car on my way to an awards after-party.

Marianne x

PS Would you like me to get tickets for you and your friend to go see On the Rox? They're playing in April. Let me know.

From: anna_huntley@zingmail.co.uk
To: marianne@montaines.co.uk
Subject: Re: Hi

Hey, Marianne!

Thanks so much for the advice. I would LOVE to take Jess to On the Rox, thank you!

Have fun at the after-party, sounds like a hoot!

Love, me xxx

From: jess.delby@zingmail.co.uk

To: anna_huntley@zingmail.co.uk

Subject: Yo!

How was your dinner?

What are you doing tomorrow? My parents want to go to this really boring exhibit. Think it has rotting animal parts involved.

Want to come?

J x

From: anna_huntley@zingmail.co.uk

To: jess.delby@zingmail.co.uk

Subject: Re: Yo!

Wow, you've really sold that exhibit to me. Actually, Sophie left me the most random voice mail about joining them in the park tomorrow, so I was thinking of going. You want to come? Should be better than a boring exhibit, right?

Love, me xxx

From: jess.delby@zingmail.co.uk

To: anna_huntley@zingmail.co.uk

Subject: Re: Yo!

She called you? And invited you to the park? That girl is on a mission. I'll pass if you don't mind. Don't think hanging out with Sophie on the weekend is really my thing.

Are you sure you want to do that?

J x

From: anna_huntley@zingmail.co.uk

To: jess.delby@zingmail.co.uk

Subject: Re: Yo!

Why wouldn't I want to do that? HELLO. Brendan is going to be there. Potentially doing something cool like skateboarding or playing soccer.

You sure you don't want to come?

Love, me xxx

From: jess.delby@zingmail.co.uk

To: anna_huntley@zingmail.co.uk

Subject: Try not to drool

It's 50 degrees outside at the moment. And windy. I wonder why Sophie invited you? Just be careful, Anna, you know what she's like.

J x

From: anna_huntley@zingmail.co.uk

To: jess.delby@zingmail.co.uk

Subject: Re: Try not to drool

No, what is she like?

Love, me xxx

From: jess.delby@zingmail.co.uk

To: anna_huntley@zingmail.co.uk

Subject: Re: Try not to drool

She likes attention. I just hope that she's not trying to latch on to this It Girl thing. You know, now you know someone famous? It's the sort of thing she loves. Be careful with that group. I don't want any of them to hurt you.

J x

From: anna_huntley@zingmail.co.uk

To: jess.delby@zingmail.co.uk

Subject: I hear ya

Okay, wise Gandalf, I will be careful.

Now, stop being grumpy and serious.

I have some news that will cheer you up.

Love, me xxx

From: jess.delby@zingmail.co.uk

To: anna_huntley@zingmail.co.uk

Subject: Re: I hear ya

Mysterious. What?

J x

From: anna_huntley@zingmail.co.uk

To: jess.delby@zingmail.co.uk

Subject: Get excited

You're going to see On the Rox in April.

Love, me xxx

From: jess.delby@zingmail.co.uk

To: anna_huntley@zingmail.co.uk

Subject: Re: Get excited

ARE YOU SERIOUS????

EEEEEEEEEEEEEEEEEEEEEEEEEEEEEEEEEE!!!!!

THIS IS THE BEST DAY EVER!!!

THANK YOU THANK YOU THANK YOU THANK YOU!

I'm super happy! You are a great best friend!

Did Marianne offer them?

J x

From: anna_huntley@zingmail.co.uk

To: jess.delby@zingmail.co.uk

Subject: Re: Get excited

Thought you might be happy about that one.

Yes she did.

I think I may have had a small breakthrough with Marianne today, you know. She almost smiled at me.

So now she's patted Dog on the head and almost smiled at me AND offered On the Rox tickets, I would say . . . we're basically best friends.

Love, me xxx

From: jess.delby@zingmail.co.uk

To: anna_huntley@zingmail.co.uk

Subject: Re: Get excited

Um. Yeah. Sure. I'm sure you guys are like best friends.

J x

From: anna_huntley@zingmail.co.uk

To: jess.delby@zingmail.co.uk

Subject: I see how it is

Don't think I can't sense that tone of sarcasm.

She gave me boy tips too, so there. A true sign of sisterhood. Do you think it's embarrassing that in an e-mail I just sent her I used the word "hoot"? That's a cool word, right? Everyone uses that word.

Love, me xxx

From: jess.delby@zingmail.co.uk

To: anna_huntley@zingmail.co.uk

Subject: Re: I see how it is

No one uses that word. This is like the time you kept trying to get the word "hullabaloo" into conversations.

Why do you need boy tips? You're so good at that sort of thing.

J x

From: anna_huntley@zingmail.co.uk
To: jess.delby@zingmail.co.uk
Subject: Re: I see how it is
Any more sarcasm and I'm giving the On the Rox tickets to Dog.
He is very partial to rock music.
Once, I put on "Bohemian Rhapsody," and he howled along to it so loudly that it gave next door's hamster a heart attack.
Love, me xxx

From: jess.delby@zingmail.co.uk
To: anna_huntley@zingmail.co.uk
Subject: Forgive me?
I take it back. All I want in life is those tickets.
You're the best best friend ever, thank you!
Just out of interest, when I called you "best friend" in that previous e-mail, did you get up and do a weird celebratory dance?
J x

From: anna_huntley@zingmail.co.uk
To: jess.delby@zingmail.co.uk

Subject: Re: Forgive me?

No?

Love, me xxx

From: jess.delby@zingmail.co.uk

To: anna_huntley@zingmail.co.uk

Subject: Re: Forgive me?

Liar. I bet you did a celebratory dance and then went to tell Dog. Am I right?

J x

From: anna_huntley@zingmail.co.uk

To: jess.delby@zingmail.co.uk

Subject: Re: Forgive me?

HOW ARE YOU DOING THIS?

Love, me xxx

From: rebecca.blythe@bouncemail.co.uk

To: anna_huntley@zingmail.co.uk

Subject: Camels

Greetings, my only child!

Looking forward to seeing you very soon during break. I've missed you!

Anyway, I wanted to let you know that I've sold you to a lovely fellow here for the excellent price of three camels. Now, I know that seems quite low, and my colleague has managed to wrangle six for his daughter, but the camels I'm looking at are of much better breeding, so they're really worth triple his.

Hope all is well, darling!

Mom xxx

From: anna_huntley@zingmail.co.uk
To: rebecca.blythe@bouncemail.co.uk
Subject: Re: Camels

Hi, Mom,

Thanks for sending me an e-mail purely to let me know how many camels I'm worth.

I am saving e-mails like this one in a special file for when I'm admitted to a mental institution.

Love, me xxx

From: rebecca.blythe@bouncemail.co.uk
To: anna_huntley@zingmail.co.uk
Subject: Re: Camels

Good for you, darling!

Now, tell me your gossip—have you got a date for the dance yet? I bet the boys are falling over themselves.

Mom xxx

From: anna_huntley@zingmail.co.uk
To: rebecca.blythe@bouncemail.co.uk
Subject: Re: Camels

Mom, this is me we're talking about remember? You seem to have me confused with someone who is popular. No, I don't have a date to the dance yet. Who on earth would I go with?

Please do not suggest Dog.

Love, me xxx

From: rebecca.blythe@bouncemail.co.uk
To: anna_huntley@zingmail.co.uk
Subject: Stop this negativity

What about that lovely boy you mentioned on the phone? Boursin or something.

Mom xxx

From: anna_huntley@zingmail.co.uk
To: rebecca.blythe@bouncemail.co.uk
Subject: Re: Stop this negativity

Mom. Boursin is a CHEESE.

His name is Brendan. And he's the most popular and best-looking guy in school. So he won't be taking me.

Love, me xxx

From: rebecca.blythe@bouncemail.co.uk
To: anna_huntley@zingmail.co.uk
Subject: Re: Stop this negativity
Why not?
I thought you said you had made some new friends this semester. So you are popular too.
Is he going with someone else?
Mom xxx

From: anna_huntley@zingmail.co.uk
To: rebecca.blythe@bouncemail.co.uk
Subject: Re: Stop this negativity
Well, no actually. He hasn't actually asked Sophie yet as far as I know. But I'm sure he will. It makes sense that they would go together. But he did call me smart yesterday. Could you imagine? If he took me to the dance, everyone would like me . . . and Jess and Danny would be pretty excited. It would definitely solve all my problems!
But it's never going to happen, Mom.
Thanks anyway.
Love, me xxx

From: rebecca.blythe@bouncemail.co.uk
To: anna_huntley@zingmail.co.uk
Subject: Excuse you, young lady
You're not getting out of it that easily, miss. He called you SMART. Boys like smart girls. They have something to talk about with them.
Maybe the reason he hasn't asked this Sophie is because he wants to ask YOU. Hmm? Have you thought of it that way? You work your magic, darling–you may get your bookish nature from your father, but you get your flair from me. It's an irresistible combination.
See you at break. I'm going to bring you back a wonderful present–and don't worry, it won't be a mug like last time.
Mom xxx

From: anna_huntley@zingmail.co.uk
To: rebecca.blythe@bouncemail.co.uk
Subject: Re: Excuse you, young lady
Mom. Let's just clarify. You brought me back a MONKEY SKULL.
Just because it had a handle glued to it does

NOT make it a mug. I don't care what that guy at the stall told you.
Please don't bring anything weird back for me.
This year has already been disturbing enough.
Love, me xxx

"Brendan is such a show-off." Sophie laughed, perching her sunglasses on her head and waving at him as he looked in our direction after scoring a second goal.

I held on tight to Dog's leash as he whined hysterically, watching the soccer ball fly around the grass between the boys. When I arrived, Sophie had made a big fuss about Dog without actually touching him, and Josie just looked a little disgusted and stepped away. Brendan had greeted him like an old friend, kneeling down to give him a good scratch.

"Brendan keeps looking at you, Sophie." Josie smiled. "He's showing off because you're here."

"No, I don't think so." Sophie blushed.

"Are you two going out?" I asked carefully.

"Not yet," Josie answered for her friend. "It's obvious that Brendan likes her though. Do you think you'll see him a lot when you're doing the internship with his mom over spring break? Do you think he visits her when she's on set?"

"I thought the internship was the prize of the raffle?" I looked at them in confusion.

"It is. Josie's being presumptuous that I'll win."

"Well, you did buy about twenty tickets." Josie grinned.

"No I did not!" Sophie said, giving Josie a pointed look.

Josie smiled knowingly to herself and went back to watching the boys run around. "I didn't realize your friend Jess was really into photography," she said a few moments later, looking over at me. "Or does she just like Brendan as well?"

"I do not like Brendan! Shut up, Josie." Sophie laughed.

"No, she doesn't like Brendan either!" I replied, patting Dog's head as Sophie smiled at me. "She's really into that sort of thing . . . photography and art. An internship would be great for her. I think she'd be really good at it; she's very creative."

"I'm surprised you haven't entered the raffle, Anna. Being around people like Helena and Marianne. They must have worked with loads of famous photographers, right?" Josie asked.

"Marianne models quite a lot I think. It isn't really my thing though. Especially not fashion photography. I wouldn't have a clue! Not like Jess or you, Sophie."

"Yeah, it would be cool to be on fashion shoots," Sophie said, twirling her hair around her finger. "Brendan's mom does a lot of those. She did one for *Vogue* you know. Do you think you'll ever be in a big magazine like that, Anna?"

"No way! I'd probably always end up on their worst-dressed lists. Luckily, I'm not interesting enough to them." I laughed. Dog pulled on the leash again and barked as the ball came racing past him.

"You could make them interested in you," Josie said sweetly. "If you started dressing up and going out more with Marianne. Although Jess would probably get jealous, wouldn't she."

"Jess? I don't think so."

"Oh, Anna, of course she would!" Josie chuckled, as though she found my naïvete endearing. "You've been getting a *lot* of attention recently. It's silly that you have such little confidence in yourself. You could be very pretty if you dressed up more."

"Really? Um, thanks," I said, taken aback by what sounded like a compliment.

"Absolutely. We could show you how!" Josie continued. "But I don't think Jess likes you hanging out with us, does she? I could tell at lunchtime."

"Josie, don't be mean." Sophie sighed. "I'm sure Jess is very happy that Anna is making new friends. It's nice you're hanging out with us, Anna. It's been fun getting to know you."

"Thanks," I said uneasily. Josie's comments made me think about Jess and her reaction to the changes that have been going on. She's been very supportive, but Josie did have a point. It was a bit strange that Jess was so reluctant for me to go to the park with a new group of friends.

My uncomfortable thoughts were disturbed by Brendan, who came bounding over to us. "Anna," he said, breathing heavily from all the running. "Let Dog off the leash."

"No way." I laughed. "He would destroy that soccer ball."

"He must be dying to be let off the leash. Go on," Brendan encouraged. "It'll be funny."

I looked at the girls. Sophie shrugged. I reached forward and unclipped Dog's leash. Immediately he sped toward the soccer ball that James was dribbling and pounced on it.

He tumbled across the field, back legs and tail flying forward and over as he rolled along, and then he attempted to gnaw at the ball. But it kept rolling away from him, making him very excited. James and the others laughed and ran toward Dog, kicking the soccer ball from him and happily running away with it while Dog chased each of them in hot pursuit, occasionally managing to steal it back.

After a few minutes, Dog leaped on the ball so aggressively that it hurled away from him and into the net. "GOAL!" James cried, and everyone ran laughing toward Dog to celebrate.

"You have the most hilarious dog." Brendan laughed as he doubled over.

"He's pretty ridiculous." I shook my head, giggling.

"I'm really happy you're here, Anna," Brendan said, brushing my arm with his hand.

I blushed and watched Brendan run back across the field to join the others in chasing down Dog, who was now just sprinting around the place without a clue what was going on. Brendan tackled Dog and began scratching his stomach happily. I laughed and looked over at Sophie and Josie.

Josie was watching Sophie carefully. Sophie was watching Brendan. Neither of them were laughing.

"I'm just saying," I explained for the billionth time. "They gave me the heebie-jeebies."

Connor put his pen down thoughtfully. It was only the two of us in detention that day, and Mr. Kenton had gone to try to work the coffee machine in the teachers' lounge.

"I don't get it." He shrugged, swinging his feet up so they were resting on the table. "How does a bunch of chickens give someone . . . the heebie-jeebies?"

"Connor, don't even pretend like you don't know what I'm

talking about. You can't understand what they're saying when they do all that clucking."

"I'm not sure I understand any animal."

"But clucking is a sinister sound. Who knows what they're plotting?"

"What could they possibly be plotting?"

I ignored him. "And they have eyes on the side of their heads! That's just wrong."

"If they gave you the heebie-jeebies, then why did you go help collect the eggs?"

"I told you. I was seven years old and my parents tricked me into it. It was at one of their friends' farms. I was so afraid of the chickens that I refused to go near them to get the eggs. Dad told me to stop crying and then, to show me they weren't frightening, he went and picked one up to bring toward me. I freaked. Mom threw a bucket of water at him when we were walking back toward the house and that made me laugh. Moms always know what to do."

"It's pretty cool that your parents get along." Connor nodded.

"Yeah, I'm clucky."

He looked at me deadpan.

"Oh come on!" I exclaimed, throwing my head back. "That was such a good one!"

"It's an old one. Done before. Get some new material, Spidey."

"Well, excuse me, comedy pro; I'll try harder next time."

Connor chuckled and then got back to sketching. I narrowed my eyes at him. "When are you going to show me this new thing you're working on? You can't keep it a secret forever."

"I'll tell you what." He grinned and covered his sketchbook with his arms so I couldn't see. "I'll show you my new drawings when you show me your hip-hop moves."

I snorted. "Well, that will be never then."

"Fine with me."

"Fine."

I sighed and pretended to be engrossed in my chemistry notes. When I stealthily peeked in his direction, I could see that he was smiling to himself as he quickly moved the pencil down the page.

It was weirdly calming to watch Connor draw. I even found the sound of the pencil scratching around on the paper comforting.

I looked at the first sentence of my chemistry notes, reasoning that it was probably a bit weird to keep staring. Connor was likely to poke me in the eye with his pencil if I kept doing that.

Sodium + chlorine = sodium chloride
$2Na + Cl2 = 2NaCl$

Hmmm . . . "When are you going to let me see it?!"

"You couldn't even last two minutes. In fact I think that was just under sixty seconds."

"Fine, fine, I'll get back to my chemistry."

"Have you got to the second sentence of that page yet?" he asked, still not looking up.

WHAT IS HE DRAWING THAT NEEDS THIS MUCH ATTENTION?! It was killing me.

"I'm actually on the third paragraph."

"Don't lie, Spidey. I can tell when you're lying."

"Can I ask you something?" I put my highlighter down.

"You can't see my new work until it's finished." He sighed.

"I wasn't going to ask about that," I said smugly. "I was going to ask why you're in detention all the time. You've never actually told me."

"You've never actually told me why *you're* in detention all the time."

"Oh please," I snorted. "Everyone knows why *I'm* here."

"I guess yours was a bit more of a talking point." He smiled. "You can't guess mine?"

"Well, you're here all semester like me, so it must have been bad. Did you set fire to something too?"

He chuckled. "Nah, nothing so exciting. It was actually my drawing that got me in trouble."

"How?"

"Last semester I skipped a couple of classes when I was working on some of my characters . . . forgot to do homework because I was drawing every evening. Ms. Duke was pretty cool about it. She said if I finished my homework in detention, I could use the rest of the time to get creative."

"I've never seen you doing homework in detention."

"Maybe that's because someone is constantly asking me questions and distracting me from it."

"Please!" I exclaimed. "You are always distracting me. Today is an exception."

"Don't get touchy. It's nice to talk to someone who likes the same kind of things I do."

"Yeah," I agreed, nodding thoughtfully. "It's nice to put off going home too, sometimes."

"How's that all going by the way? The It Girl stuff?"

I shrugged. "Better. Marianne and I are actually having real conversations. Sort of. It took a little while though. We're pretty different."

"How do you mean? Does she have pet chickens?"

"Very funny. You know. Sometimes it's hard to be . . ." I hesitated, feeling embarrassed. I hadn't really spoken to anyone else about this at length before.

Connor put down his sketchbook and looked at me curiously. "Tell me."

"Well, you know—" I paused. Connor was looking at me intently. I hadn't realized quite how dark his eyes really were. Geez—why was I thinking about that? "Um, it's, well . . . um . . . really *hard* to be around people like that. Not because they're not nice or anything. Marianne seems lovely. Not that I know her that well but, you know, she seems nice. But she is also *Marianne Montaine*. Britain's perfect It Girl." I shrugged. "And I'm not."

He leaned back in his chair and picked up his sketchbook and pencil again. I looked at him, slightly confused, as he pushed the pencil back and forth. Had I bored him so much that he was just going to start drawing again?

How embarrassing. I really needed more tips from Jess about how to speak to people in public.

"I disagree."

"I'm sorry?"

"I think *you're* Britain's perfect It Girl, Spidey," Connor said seriously.

"You're teasing me again," I said grumpily. "Stop it. I was telling you personal stuff there."

"I'm not—I promise!" He laughed and went back to his sketchbook. "Don't worry. You just keep doing what you're doing. You'll get it eventually."

Right on cue Mr. Kenton came in, grumbling about stupid complicated machinery and how he doesn't understand why they couldn't just have a kettle, coffee cans, and mugs like they used to.

I shifted back in my seat and tried to concentrate on the chemistry equations in front of me, but it was really difficult—and not just because chemistry is so thrilling.

Every time I glanced over at Connor drawing, he had this mischievous grin on him. And it bothered me—I just didn't know why.

16.

THERE IS NOTHING I DREAD MORE—EXCEPT FOR sports day—than the bus rides at the beginning and end of a school trip.

No one else has to worry. Everyone else gets excited about school trips because you get to miss a day of class and you get to go somewhere new. But, for me, bus rides are merely another cause of humiliation. Like school dances, they naturally highlight the popular and the unpopular. Nothing shouts "You have no one to sit with!" louder. I have always sat on my own or, worse, up front with a teacher.

Today, on the last day before break, our grade was being taken on a field trip out in the country somewhere. That was two of my worst fears combined. Bus rides AND sports.

In theory, now that I had Jess and Danny, it might not have been so bad, but Danny gets horrifically carsick, so he had bagged Jess as his seat buddy for emotional and bag-holding support. She wasn't delighted with the responsibility for "McPukey," and it also meant that I was essentially by myself again, but at least I could try to get the seats in the row opposite them. I would have to be quick in the dog-eat-dog pile-on to the bus.

I was so nervous that not even Dog could pull me out of my slump the evening before the outing. Not that he didn't try. At one point he even brought me a frozen leg of lamb. Although amazed that he had managed to retrieve it from the freezer (seriously, HOW?!), I just couldn't feel calm.

"Don't do the activities you don't want to do," Dad had told me. "Or if you have to, then laugh at yourself. You can't expect to be good at everything."

Oh thanks so much, Dad. I don't know whether you've noticed, but, thanks to the genes you passed down to me, I happen to be good at NOTHING.

When I wouldn't cheer up, he rudely called me "a big grump," and then, as he went upstairs to get ready for bed, he asked me to remind him to get the leg of lamb out of the freezer the next morning for the dinner party he was throwing tomorrow.

I smirked at Dog. Good luck with that one, Dad. That's karma for you.

Anyway, when I stepped on to the bus the next morning, I was feeling especially nervous. I'd turned up late to school because Dad had been searching for the stupid lamb, so I totally missed the rush onto the bus. It was my usual nightmare played out all over again. At least at my last school people didn't really pay attention to me on a daily basis. At this one, I was the It Girl who still had no one to sit next to.

"Forget to set your alarm today, Spidey?" Connor smiled up at me from one of the first few rows, where he was sitting next to Max. They had both come prepared for the journey with headphones around their necks, and I could see a small sketchbook sticking out of Connor's bag.

"No, there was a . . . lamb incident." Both Connor and Max blinked up at me in confusion. "Don't worry about it," I said hurriedly. "It's not interesting."

"It sounds fascinating." He grinned. "You can sit opposite us if you like." He gestured to the next-door row, and I felt a wave of gratitude.

"I don't think so, Mr. Lawrence," came Mrs. Ginnwell's stern high-pitched tone as she scrambled onto the bus behind me with her clipboard in hand. "I'll be sitting in the row opposite you and Mr. Gelson. I don't want any trouble on this trip, and I will be keeping a close eye on both of you."

"Mrs. Ginnwell." Max feigned a dramatic sigh, lifting up his headphones. "I told you that time with the cornstarch was an accident. When are you going to start trusting me?"

She narrowed her eyes. "No time soon, Mr. Gelson."

I raised my eyebrows at Connor as Max smiled and shoved his headphones on and Mrs. Ginnwell bustled into the opposite row, almost taking me out with her clipboard.

"What happened with the cornstarch?"

"That's a story for a rainy day." Connor chuckled. He looked at me apologetically. "There's probably some spaces farther down near Jess."

Connor was right in that there was a space near Jess and Danny—in fact the row opposite them was completely empty. But as I neared it, a strange smell hit me, and the pained look on Jess's face didn't bring me much comfort. "Is that . . . Lysol?" I asked, scrunching my nose.

"Good going, Sherlock." Jess glanced at Danny, who was already resting his head on her shoulder, looking very pale, a "just in case" plastic shopping bag scrunched on his lap. His eyes were closed and his mouth very slightly hanging open. "You missed the main event. Luckily, I was still making my way to the seat. The driver only turned the engine on for like one second."

"Is he okay?"

"The nurse gave him some motion sickness tablets—I think he's got it all out now. Mrs. Ginnwell went to town on the disinfectant. It's a little overpowering, and I think the seat is still a bit damp. Sorry, Anna, I tried saving you a seat somewhere nearby but people kept nabbing them." Jess craned her neck to look at the rows behind. "I think there's a few spare seats at the back that are fairly close."

"I'll find one." I nodded, waving it off like it wasn't a big deal.

"This stinks. We'll definitely sit near each other on the way back." She kneeled up on her seat. "I'll watch for where you sit so I can come visit during the ride."

"Yeah, course." This made me feel a bit better, and I gave her what I hoped to be a brave smile before making my way farther down the bus. I spotted Sophie and Josie huddled together in the back with some other girls, laughing at something on Sophie's phone, but there were no free seats near them.

"Sit here if you like," a voice piped up as I passed. Brendan Dakers smiled up at me, leaning back against the bus window with his legs draped over both seats in his row.

I stared at him. He shrugged and swung his legs down,

leaving the aisle seat next to him empty. "If you want, this seat is free."

I glanced back at Jess, who was looking as shocked as I felt. But she nodded encouragingly toward the seat anyway.

Sophie and Josie had looked up from the phone and were watching carefully. I slid into the seat next to Brendan, trying to act as calm as possible (not very).

The journey was a long one as we drove out of London and away into the countryside. Every now and then, when Brendan got animated telling me a story, his arm would accidentally brush mine and I would forget to breathe. I tried to remember to nod and laugh in all the right places, even though most of his stories were about sports, which I didn't always understand.

When we got to the park and got off the bus, Brendan smiled and said, "See you later," then went to join James and the other soccer boys while I stumbled toward Jess and Danny.

"You okay?" Danny croaked, still clutching his plastic bag and looking green.

"I think I should be asking you that, Danny, but thanks! I can't believe I just got to sit next to Brendan Dakers. Stuff like that never happens to me."

"What did he talk about?" Jess asked curiously.

"I'm not really sure. I was concentrating too hard on being normal."

Jess nudged me, and we laughed as we hooked our arms through Danny's to lead him toward where everyone was gathering for a safety talk.

We were split into two groups, with half the grade going toward the ATV courses in the open fields and the other half, which I was standing in, toward the woods. "Good thing that you're in that group," Connor said, suddenly next to me as everyone excitedly followed the instructors. "I hear there are zip lines in the forest. You'll be right at home zipping through the air eh, Spidey?"

He winked and rushed off to join the other group.

Zip lines? I gulped.

I hurried to catch up with my group and found myself with Josie and Sophie, who were at the back and not looking very pleased with the forest we were about to enter. "That was sweet of Brendan to ask you to sit with him," Sophie observed. Josie watched me carefully.

"Yeah, I think he took pity on me," I replied quickly, chuckling.

Sophie smiled. "No, I'm sure that's not it."

We followed our group down a forest path. "Urgh," said Josie loudly, as we navigated our way down a small but steep drop, "this is so not fun. I'm not doing anything that involves wearing a harness."

"All the activities involve wearing a harness, Josie." Jess laughed over her shoulder as she climbed down after the instructor. "Unless you like free fall?"

"Well, we won't be doing them," Sophie snapped, rubbing her hands clean after gripping some dirty rocks to get down safely.

"The girls can watch." Brendan grinned.

"Thanks, Brendan, but some of us aren't scared to join in," Jess argued, folding her arms as we all gathered in a group around the instructor.

I didn't say anything.

Sophie and Josie categorically refused to go near the zip line, and, along with a couple of other girls—and Danny, who still looked very pale and sorry for himself as he sipped cautiously from a bottle of water—they sat on their jackets on some benches nearby, cheering on Brendan and his friends as they climbed up toward it.

I was more than happy to sit with them, but Jess can be very persuasive when she wants to be. "You'll enjoy it, I promise," she said, gripping my arm. "Please do it with me."

"Okay, fine." I sighed, reaching for a very unattractive red helmet. She was so pleased that she jumped up and down on the spot. Sophie and Josie watched with a grimace as one of the guides strapped me into a harness and attached me to a wire, instructing me to climb up the pole to the top, where the other instructor was waiting.

My confidence faded very quickly when I got to the top and looked down. I immediately regretted listening to Jess, who had gone before me and was now standing at the other side waving encouragingly. I gulped.

"Go on, Anna!" Brendan yelled from below, where he was sitting with Sophie after having had his turn.

Realizing I couldn't back out now, I leaped off the side and flew across. It was terrifying but actually exhilarating as well, and as I reached the end, I heard Brendan and the others whoop loudly.

I was so thrilled at everyone cheering that I welled up a little as I climbed down. "See?" Jess cried when I got to the bottom, helping me take my helmet off and giving me a massive hug. "You enjoyed it, right?"

"Yes, but no more scary activities for me." I laughed. "All right?"

"Absolutely," Jess nodded. "I'm so proud of you."

"Me too," Danny said, slowly coming over to pat me on the back as though that was a huge amount of effort.

Toward the end of the day the two groups joined back together and, utterly worn out, we were taken to the edge of the woods, which was lined by some rocks, where the stream from the woods became a small waterfall that splashed down the side and into caves. Sophie, Josie, and a group of girls had already set up camp around some benches. "Right," began the instructor. "Anyone with enough energy left who wants to explore the caves can rappel down. If not, you can wait by the benches."

Sophie and Josie didn't even look up, they were in such deep conversation about something on their phones. Intrigued by what they were talking about and completely exhausted, I slouched toward them.

"Anna, can you come with me?" I looked around to see Jess holding two helmets.

"No, no, no." I smiled at her. "I don't want to rappel into dark, murky caves thank you."

"Please, Anna," she pleaded, dropping the helmets to her sides in defeat.

"Take Danny," I said, gesturing to him. He was sitting

on one of the benches, clutching his plastic bag.

"Is he *still* not better?" I huffed, realizing what this probably meant.

Jess looked at me pleadingly. "Pleeeeease, no other girls will come. You'll enjoy it; it'll be like an adventure. I'll be scared on my own!"

"You won't be on your own," Josie said, obviously listening to our conversation. Jess and I turned to see the group of girls watching us. "All the boys are going."

"I know," Jess said, looking at her feet. "But it would be nice if I had another girl with me. Sisterhood and girl power and all of that. Heard of it, Josie?"

Josie scowled in response.

I noticed for the first time that, despite the front she was putting up, Jess looked nervous. I don't think I've ever seen Jess look nervous before. I took one of the helmets. "I'll come with you." I gulped.

She looked at me in surprise, her eyes filled with gratitude. "Really?"

"Really?" Sophie repeated.

"Yeah," I said, my voice wobbling slightly. "It'll be fun."

"Anna." Josie sighed. "If I were you, I wouldn't. It's not very cool. Come and sit with us."

I took a deep breath. "It's okay. We'll come over after."

"Um, *you* can," Jess muttered under her breath. I gave her a look, and she had the good grace to give me an apologetic smile. I put on the helmet and walked toward the edge. Josie leaned in toward Sophie and whispered something to her as the instructor tightened the harness around the top of my legs.

I shuffled about with the strap around my waist, trying to make my harness a bit more comfortable, when Connor came over. He was strapped up for the rappel too. "You don't have to do this if you don't want to," he said quietly. "People won't care. Do what you want to do."

"I don't mind. Jess is all excited," I said by way of explanation and then attempted to tuck my top back into my harness as it kept rising up. "I'm sure it will be fine."

"Yeah, well I hear you've at least tackled a few of the activities today, unlike some people." He rolled his eyes toward Sophie, who was debriefing Josie on all her break plans. "Apparently you're a dark horse on an ATV."

"Okay, firstly, I do not appreciate your sarcasm, and secondly, I swear someone must have moved that stack of tires to the middle of the track for my turn."

"See you down there, Spidey." He grinned and joined the line of rappelers. I waited for Jess before attempting to walk after him as elegantly as possible while wearing a safety harness.

It was not an easy task.

The boys had made their way down, and it was Jess's turn. She looked nervous leaning over the edge, but she navigated her way down quickly, laughing about her sneakers getting wet in the water. "Come on, Anna, it's easy! You'll love it!" she yelled up. I peered over and saw Brendan standing next to her, giving me the thumbs-up. Connor was next to Max, away from the rest of the group. He nodded at me encouragingly.

"Ready, Anna?" the instructor, Evan, asked as he signaled to the other guide below.

"No." I shook my head.

"You're completely safe," he said softly so only I could hear. "Just go as slow as you like, one step at a time. I've got you."

I took a deep breath and, trying to act like I was very cool and collected like Jess, I leaned slowly backward. "That's it." Evan smiled. "Perfect. Now off you go—pop that left foot into the first hold. Can you see that dip there? Take your time."

I did as I was told and placed my shaking leg down into the hold. Then I did the same with the right. Suddenly I felt a rush of confidence. Feeling the harness tighten, I felt safe with

Evan holding on. I cautiously began to descend backward, my canvas sneakers slowly becoming soaked as I found each foothold next to the gentle waterfall.

I knew I was getting near the end when I could hear Jess shouting up kind words of encouragement. Feeling braver, I sped up, taking step after step down. I started to enjoy it and thought happily about how the guys below must be pretty impressed. I wondered if Brendan was still watching.

And then I got truly stuck.

I realized I had put my right foot into a hole that was much too small, and somehow my foot was wedged in. I tried to shake my leg free, but my sneaker wouldn't budge. I knew Evan had me on the rope, so slowly I let go of the side and attempted to pull out my foot using both hands.

Evan continued to lower the rope that was holding up my body, not able to see this far down. Suddenly my upper body dropped backward and my foot remained stuck, the safety rope around my waist.

I was hanging upside down in a small waterfall.

Flailing around wildly, I couldn't see or hear anything because of the noise of the water. And then when it seemed like the situation couldn't get any more dire, my sweater fell loose from the harness and dropped down over my face.

As I hung upside down, having remembered the Wolverine thermal underwear I was wearing (that Dad had insisted on for the cold weather) was on display for everyone to see, I genuinely wished I could stay there until everyone else went home.

Eventually though, I was lowered to the bottom, where the second instructor grabbed hold of me half laughing as he unclipped the rope and checked if I was all right.

I looked up and saw Sophie, Josie, and the other girls gathered around the edge and looking down, their hands over their mouths, some of them giggling. I stood there, totally drenched, wiping the water off my face.

Someone took my hand, and I turned my head to see Connor Lawrence by my side. "Anna, are you all right?"

"I'm fine. Please don't make a fuss," I whispered, completely mortified that everyone was still laughing at me. Out of the corner of my eye I could see Brendan Dakers and the other boys watching us.

Connor followed my eyeline over to Brendan and pulled his hand away. "Fine." He walked off toward the back of the cave wall.

"Oh, Con–" I began, but was interrupted as Jess ran over looking upset. "Anna! Oh my goodness, are you okay?"

I looked around to try to catch Connor's eye, but he was resolutely facing the other way. Brendan was still watching though. I shook my head. "No, Jess," I replied, my eyes welling up.

Jess gave me a big hug and then squeezed the bottom of my sweater to wring it out.

"Did it look awful?"

"No, it wasn't that bad," she replied carefully before letting out a small, apologetic giggle. "I mean, it was a little funny to watch. You know, you were sort of swaying upside down in the water. Don't worry though, I made sure no one filmed it on their phone . . . Nice thermal underwear, by the way."

So everyone had seen it.

"Did Brendan see?" I hissed desperately.

"Uh." She bit her nail. "Well, I think so. You know, everyone was looking up to watch you come down. . . . But I doubt anyone thought it was a big deal; I mean Brendan was laughing. You know, um, in a nice way."

I pushed my sopping hair off my face. I knew Jess was being kind, but even she must have been embarrassed by that. I wondered what she was really thinking.

I sat on the bus on the way home, wrapped in a towel and on my own again. Even if Brendan hadn't been sitting with Sophie, Josie, and the popular crowd, I was far too ashamed to sit next to him after today. Connor was sitting in the front again but hadn't said anything when I walked past.

I listened to Jess and Danny laughing in the seats opposite, the chatter of Sophie and Brendan as they flirted in the back seats, and the forced laughter of Josie as one of the soccer players told her an unfunny joke, and I made the decision there and then that things were going to change. I no longer wanted to be Anna Huntley, the embarrassing geek who wore Wolverine thermal underwear and couldn't do anything right.

I looked out of the window and made a pact with myself. I had to become someone who wouldn't be an embarrassment to spend time with. I'd be someone everyone would admire and, ultimately, someone they might even want to be.

I had to become Anna Huntley, the It Girl.

TEN REASONS WHY MY PARENTS COULD NEVER BE together although they would never admit any of these:

1. My mom talks to Dog in a baby voice. My dad HATES this. "For goodness' sake, Rebecca, he's not a replacement child. If you feel the need to speak in that manner, go to the local nursery and volunteer. Don't torture my poor Labrador."
2. My dad talks to Dog like he is a fellow member in a renowned gentlemen's club. My mom HATES this. "For goodness' sake, Nicholas, he doesn't care whether it's a 'voluminous' port and he certainly won't join you for a cigar. Make new friends."
3. Mom doesn't like silence so makes little clicking sounds with her tongue every now and then

during long periods of quiet. These sounds make Dad dig his fingernails into his leg.

4. The last time my mom stayed at our house, she painted one of the doors orange when Dad was out at a meeting because she said the house was: "Like your father, looking dreary." Neither the orange nor the reason behind it went down well.

5. Dad eats very quickly and then gets the hiccups. Every meal, Mom says, "Slow down, Nick; at your age you'll get heartburn," to which he replies, "Leave me alone; I'm enjoying my food." And then he gets the hiccups. She gets very angered by this process each time it happens. Then they have a conversation that in theory is with me, but actually they don't even look at me once. Just give each other death stares. "He never listens to me, Anna!" "I would listen to her, Anna, if she didn't tell me how to behave all the time. Please remind your mother that I'm a grown man!"

6. My mom backed his new Volvo into a mailbox. And then a bread van. And then the side of

the garage where she took it to be fixed.
7. My dad took her new Audi for a test drive and totaled it.
8. Every time she comes to stay, my mom throws out any of Dad's clothes or shoes she doesn't approve of but doesn't tell him. Most of the time he only realizes a few weeks after she's gone, when he's late for something and is looking for his "darned green bow tie." Then I get: "Anna. Please get your mother on the phone, NOW. I don't care if she's trekking in the Andes. I said NOW."
9. They constantly bicker over which newscaster is the best on TV.
10. They both hate that the other one knows them better than they know themselves.

Mom arrived on Monday laden with gifts from around the world. "What a lovely fruit bowl," my dad said grimly, trying to sound enthusiastic as he held it out away from him.

"It's not a fruit bowl, Nick." Mom laughed. "It's a hat! Put it on, it will go so well with your bow tie collection. You can wear it when we go for that expensive meal you promised me about nine years ago."

Luckily I did not receive any animal bones this year and was instead pleased to be given some very pretty jewelry. "You can wear this necklace and feel brave," my mom said gently, holding out an amber pendant.

When she had finished making herself at home, which involved scattering bright and colorful patterned throws from Peru across all the sofas, beds, and chairs in the house, we sat down with a cup of tea, and I filled her in on everything that had happened that semester.

Dad huffily went about the house removing all the throws and clearing up the mess Mom had already made in the bathroom, and then joined us just as I was elaborating on the events of the school trip, placing great focus on the thermal underwear situation.

"So as you can see, either I need to make a big change, or I need to leave the country. I can't go back to school without doing anything." I sighed dramatically.

"I see." My mom placed her teacup down onto the saucer. "Well, I take it you won't be leaving the country anytime soon, otherwise Dog would be at a loss, so what are you thinking for the big change?"

I shrugged. "I've got a few ideas. But that's where I need your advice. Dad is no help."

"Hey!" Dad said, shuffling round in the armchair. "I keep receiving these unjust accusations. I helped with the boy advice, didn't I?"

"Dad, I told you; I can't go around cooking steaks at school."

My mom looked confused. "What does steak have to do with boy troubles?"

"A lot apparently." I rolled my eyes and reached for a cookie.

"I don't see why you have to make any changes," Dad stated grumpily. "You're perfect just as you are. You can't stop being you."

"Unfortunately not, but I can stop being so *obviously* me."

"What on earth does that mean?" he asked, looking at Mom for help. She shrugged.

"None of your business," I said curtly. "But I have enlisted the help of Helena and Marianne. Both of whom will be meeting us for lunch today."

"I didn't know about this."

"You're not invited, Dad. Girls only. Mom, we're meeting them at one thirty."

"I don't see why I can't come," Dad huffed, looking very disgruntled.

"Because I need you to approve of the end results. But it wouldn't be right for you to witness the process," I explained.

Dad looked baffled, and Mom laughed out loud. "I'm sorry, Nick, looks like you're on your own this afternoon. Isn't our daughter a hoot!"

Ah. That's where I inherited that word from.

"She's certainly a lot of things," he muttered, furrowing his eyebrows.

We met Helena and Marianne at the hairdresser that Helena had recommended. I didn't consider until we were there that I maybe should have let my dad introduce his future wife to the mother of his only child, but I needn't have worried. Mom and Helena immediately hit it off. I think my dad may have a type: beautiful, headstrong, and ever-so-slightly crazy.

They sat down on the sofa together with their glasses of champagne and talked without interruption about travels, film sets, movie stars, children, and my dad. The only time they stopped to pay attention to anyone else was when the hairdresser, Burt, ran his fingers through my long, flat, mousey-brown hair. "I think bangs. And I think auburn. Marianne?"

Marianne, who had stepped back somewhat while our

moms loudly and excitedly got to know each other, was now confident and in her comfort zone. She moved forward to stand next to Burt and scrutinize my reflection. "I think you're right," she said, taking a handful of my hair and holding it up in the light. "I think red would suit her skin tone. And bangs would bring out her lovely eyes."

I flushed at the compliment, but Marianne was too distracted by my split ends to notice. Helena and Mom did that thing that only moms can do, which is tilt their head and make an "aw" expression without actually saying anything. They both did it. I saw them in the mirror.

"Are you sure about this, Anna?" Marianne suddenly asked, gently letting down my hair and taking me by surprise.

"Yes. Why?"

"You don't need to change what you look like to try to please everyone else," she said matter-of-factly. "It's hard work. That's what I have to do every day. It's not you."

"I want it to be me though." I sighed. "I'm tired of being sad when I see myself."

"All right then," Marianne said. "As long as you're sure you're doing it for the right reasons. Let's find you some more confidence."

And with that she gave the go-ahead to Burt with a nod. He

pulled his tray of instruments and bottles of color toward him. "Let's get to work," he announced dramatically, pinging the end of the disposable glove he had just put on with a flourish.

Gulp.

I sat quietly while he mixed the color and began to twist locks of my hair up to be clipped on the top of my head. Mom and Helena were giggling on the sofa over a story that Helena was retelling, and Marianne sat patiently in the chair next to mine, flicking through a magazine.

I let Burt push my head at awkward angles and smother it in strong-smelling goo. "Why the change?" he asked suddenly, rubbing the color to the ends of my hair.

"I've embarrassed myself and my friends too many times," I explained. "I want things to be different."

"Hair is a great place to start." Burt nodded. "Marianne has done that a million times."

"I have not!" She swiveled in her chair to face us. "I just get bored with my hair color."

"Mmm," Burt said knowingly. "Funny how you get bored with your hair color whenever some scandal about you comes out in the papers."

"Completely coincidental." Marianne smirked.

Burt chuckled, finished rubbing brown liquid in my hair,

and then said it was time to wait for the color to set in. "I'll leave you ladies to it, and I'll come back and have a look in a minute. Meanwhile, Marianne, why don't you tell Anna here about the scandal that came out right before you dyed *your* hair auburn." He flounced off giggling.

"What? What happened?" I asked eagerly.

"I believe Burt is referring to the time that I drove a golf cart into a lake," she replied, examining her makeup in the mirror. "Or he might be talking about the time I went a slightly brighter auburn, and that was after I lost my house key and tried climbing over a wall. Two tips for you in that situation. Don't climb a wall when there are photographers around, and it's a good idea to disable the security system."

"That was quite a fine you landed me," Helena piped up, holding out her glass for a refill of champagne and graciously thanking the assistant who poured it. "Wasting police time."

"Wow." I nodded. "Now I feel really boring."

"You're only twelve, right?" Marianne shrugged. "There's still time."

Mom and I sat enthralled as Helena launched into a series of scandalous tales about her many costars of the past with commentary from Marianne. By the time Burt came back to check on how things were coming along, we were all in fits of giggles as Helena re-enacted a moment on a movie set when an actor, furious at his lines being cut, proposed a fencing duel with the director.

Burt attempted to examine my head as I shook with laughter and then put a hand in the air to demand quiet. "To the sink!"

My hair has never experienced so many products as Burt scrubbed and rinsed, before blasting the hair dryer at me. Then there was more combing, some hair spray, a rather uncomfortable moment when I couldn't see anything as he pushed my hair down over my face to create bangs, and suddenly everyone was quiet.

"Well, Anna?" Burt took a step back and wiped his forehead with the back of his hand. "What do you think?"

For a moment I couldn't say anything because there was a girl looking back at me in the mirror that I didn't even recognize. My auburn hair was glossy, *really* glossy, like Marianne's. And it actually had volume, framing my face rather than hanging limply around it. My eyes peeked out from under the bangs and somehow they looked bigger and brighter. I looked . . . *nice.*

"It's amazing the difference a simple haircut can make." Marianne smiled gently at me.

"Simple?" Burt huffed. "Great artists *make* it look easy."

"Darling, you look just stunning!" Mom said, choking back tears. "So grown-up!"

"Burt, you really are a genius," Helena gushed. "You look beautiful, Anna."

"Well"—Burt smiled kindly at me in the mirror—"it helps when your model has the raw material."

"Now," Helena said, clapping her hands excitedly, "shopping time!"

"Excellent idea, Helena." Mom jumped up. "Lead the way!"

As the two of them started mapping out the shops we needed to visit and how many days they would need to get around them all, Marianne looked very amused.

"Looks like we're in for an interesting week."

I stared back at my reflection and nodded. "Yeah. Looks like it."

By the end of break I had been to so many stores, and been primped and preened by so many people, that I wondered how anyone managed to look this prepared all the time. Celebrities must feel constantly exhausted by everything that goes on to make them look naturally good. Friday was the biggest day of all, because Marianne had invited me to a premiere.

She even let me come to her house first to have my makeup done, and her stylist was going to help me pick out a dress from her collection. Dad was so ecstatic that Marianne and I were going to be getting ready together that he stopped whining about how I was changing too much and growing up too fast. Instead he kept going on about how nice it was that we were "bonding" and played Billy Joel at full volume as he drove me over to their house, singing along and bopping his shoulders. When "Uptown Girl" came on I thought he was going to explode with joy. I had to tell him to calm down as I didn't want him to have an aneurysm or anything.

Even Mom in the front seat was slightly disconcerted by his behavior. "Honestly, Nicholas, I haven't see you this smug since you interviewed Paul McCartney."

He wasn't the only one. Helena had organized snacks that would have fed a small nation, and their entire living room had been transformed into our dressing room. I looked through the clothes racks that were dotted around the room in awe. "We have some ideas for you, so you can pick the one you like the most," Cat, Marianne's smiley stylist with pink dip-dyed hair, informed me as she started pulling dresses out of the mass. "But I think Marianne has one that she thinks you'll particularly like."

"Yeah I do." Marianne came traipsing down the stairs and into the room, her hair in curlers, wearing a white bathrobe that had a gold embroidered "M" on it. On her feet were really big . . . *Winnie the Pooh slippers*?

Wait a moment.

"Marianne!" I blurted out before I could think. "What are those?" I pointed at her footwear.

"What? They're slippers." She shrugged and stuck out a foot. "What's wrong with them?"

"They're big Winnie the Pooh faces. On your feet."

"What's your point here?"

Oh ho ho. How the tables had turned.

"Marianne." I smirked. "You are a secret nerd."

"What?" She glanced in a panic at Cat. "No I'm not."

"Yeah you are!" I beamed. "You are a nerd! You have Winnie the Pooh slippers!"

"I'm not a nerd!"

"I have to say, you had me fooled. I thought that we were not of the same ilk, but . . ." I reached into the tote bag I had brought with me and dramatically whipped out a pair of Eeyore slippers. "I was wrong."

"Oh my goodness!" Helena cried from the doorway. "You are matching!"

Marianne looked from me to her mother and back at me again. Before she burst into laughter. "What can I say?" She grinned, reaching for a clothes bag hanging on one of the racks. "Geek chic?"

Helena scuttled off excitedly to get my parents and inform them of the slipper revelation while Marianne held up a navy blue long silk dress. "This will suit you—try it on."

I'd never seen anything so beautiful and was happy just to stare at the dress on the hanger, but Marianne was being all bossy and made Cat get me into it before I even got to inspect it properly.

"Go on, go on," Marianne said, herding me toward the full-length mirror when Cat had finished fussing and making her last adjustments.

I held up the dress around my ankles so I didn't trip and shuffled over to the mirror, making a mental note to practice walking like a normal person before we left. I felt like a five-year-old who had raided her mother's wardrobe—until I looked up into the mirror.

I was so surprised that I did a little gasp that made Cat and Marianne exchange a smug glance. The silky dress fell down from the tiny jeweled spaghetti straps like a waterfall, just skimming the floor. And its deep navy hue was the color of midnight. I couldn't stop looking at it.

"Well? What do you think?" Marianne asked.

"I feel like a movie star," I breathed, twirling around and watching the dress catch the light from all different angles.

"We haven't finished with you yet," Marianne stated as Cat came over to help me reluctantly step out of the dress so that a nice makeup artist named Taylor, who had been in the kitchen chatting with Dad about great places to go fishing, could sort out my face and hair.

When both our makeup and hair were done, Marianne ordered everyone out of the room.

"No need to be quite so controlling, darling. You really are becoming more and more like me every day," Helena grumbled as she was sent to the kitchen, having been admiring the whole process with my mother from the sofa.

"So they can see the full effect as we emerge," Marianne explained once they had all filed out. "I'll help you into your dress."

She zipped me up and then let me put on my shoes and jewelry before she took a step back, and with her hands on her hips, said, "All right then. Show me your pose."

"My what?"

"Your pose."

"I have a pose?"

"You have to have a pose. For all the photographers. That's why we're going."

"We're going for the film," I said pointedly.

"No one goes for the film apart from nerds. Oh yeah, for a second I forgot who I was talking to. Okay, I guess you're going for the film." She raised her eyebrows. "Go on then."

"Go on what?!"

"Your POSE. Pretend I'm a photographer . . . and go."

I took a moment to think about it.

"Come on!"

"All *RIGHT*. Keep your slippers on."

I struck a pose. Marianne paused.

"I'm sorry, did I ask you to do an impression of a goose?"

"I was doing an impression of a goose?"

"It's the first animal that came to my head when I saw you. Definite resemblance." Marianne nodded gravely.

"I didn't know I could do a goose."

"Focus, Anna. Shoulders back, head up, one arm on your hip, the other by your side, one leg slightly in front of the other one, elongated, head slightly tilted," Marianne reeled off as I desperately tried to keep up with her instructions.

She paused to look at me. "You look ridiculous." She sighed and came over to rearrange limbs, poking me all over the place and moving my head around.

She pushed my shoulders back, kicked my ankle so that I moved my leg forward, and then she took a step back to admire her handiwork. "Something is missing."

"My ankle bone?" I scowled.

"Ah!" She winked at me. "Remember to smile."

I grimaced, my ankle still smarting.

"What is that?! You're flirting with the camera, not taking it on in a fight."

I laughed.

"Perfect! Anna Huntley, you look like an It Girl."

I beamed.

"Are you ready?" she asked, leading me past our cooing parents and to the front door, where a limousine was waiting.

I nodded. Time to change.

18.

ANNA PAINTS THE TOWN RED!

By Nancy Rose—*The Daily Post*

Red is the color of the season according to new girl about town, Anna Huntley. This weekend the twelve-year-old was out in London attending the movie premiere of *You and I* and took the opportunity to show off her brand-new look. Sporting glossy red locks, Anna arrived with Marianne Montaine wearing a figure-hugging Alexander McQueen dress, accessorized with Tiffany's bangles and a statement Topshop necklace. She may be a lot younger than her soon-to-be stepsister, but she showed that she can make waves just as big. We love Anna's new look! Do you? Rate it out of five below.

WHAT AN(NA) IT GIRL!

By Hannah Lightly—*Entertainment Daily*

Spotted: the Montaines showing the newest addition to their family how it's done! Actress Helena Montaine and her daughter Marianne have been out and about this week with Anna Huntley, the daughter of Helena's journalist fiancé, Nicholas. It looks like Anna has been picking up style tips from those in the know, as we caught them enjoying a lovely day on London's Bond Street laden down with shopping bags. Despite shying away from attention in recent weeks, it looks like Anna is beginning to embrace the It Girl lifestyle . . . and with a family like the Montaines guiding her, who can blame her? Enjoy some of Marianne's and Anna's looks this week in our photo montage on the next page.

SISTER SISTER!

By Tammy May—*Stylish Online*

We were thrilled this week to see Marianne Montaine and the usually camera-shy Anna Huntley, the daughter of Helena Montaine's fiancé, bonding over some extreme shopping, but things got even more adorable when a few days later Anna accompanied her future stepsister to the premere of a new film. We caught up with Ms. Huntley as she entered the theater and asked if she was excited about the evening. She replied that she was "simply honored to be here with Marianne." Everyone together now, aww . . .

"Wow. You look amazing, Anna. I didn't know you were doing this!" Jess ran up to me at my locker and gave me a big hug. We hadn't seen each other over break, as Marianne had organized a whirlwind of social engagements for us to get the new me out there for everyone to see. It had been exhausting and I had missed Jess and Danny, but I knew it would be easier for them when the new shiny me turned up at school and not the old Anna who had led them from one embarrassment to another.

I put my hand up to my hair self-consciously. "Do you like it, really?"

"Really. But then I also liked the old you too. But seriously, you look great."

I grinned, happy at Jess's approval. "I missed you over break."

"Geek." She blushed. "But I missed you too, Ms. Social Butterfly. Luckily I was fairly busy too—I went to this amazing magazine photography exhibition. It made me feel quite excited. I think you were right, Anna; I really like the idea of it."

"That's great, Jess," I enthused. "I really hope you get that internship in the raffle."

"Well, the chances are slim, and that's all down to luck." She shrugged. "But Mom said she might get me a real professional camera if I do win it. And I was thinking, even if I don't, maybe I could write a letter to Brendan's mom asking for experience next summer. Or maybe your dad knows someone?" She looked sheepish. "Or Marianne might have a photographer friend?"

"Of course, that's a great idea. I can ask them."

"Would you, Anna? That would be so great!" Jess seemed so happy, and I felt a big rush of relief. I had been nervous about going back to school and seeing Jess. She'd been really kind on e-mail about the rappelling disaster, but I knew it must have been embarrassing for her. It felt like the new me was starting to pay off already.

"Wow."

We both turned to see Brendan standing there.

It was the exact reaction I had been hoping for. I looked at Jess and grinned.

"You look great, Anna." He smiled. "Big change."

"Sure is," Jess said, watching him carefully.

"I saw you in the papers," he said. "Must be pretty cool to go to stuff like that. Was the movie good?"

I nodded, my mouth feeling very dry. Luckily Jess doesn't completely lose her head when a boy talks to her. "She said it was really funny," Jess prompted me.

"It was very funny," I repeated.

"Nice," Brendan replied. We stood there for a little longer, me trying to think of something good to say and failing, Jess watching me with interest. "Well," he said eventually, "better go to class."

"See you." Jess shook her head as he strolled off. "Well, you handled that well."

"Was it really awkward? Was I embarrassing? Why will no one tell me what to say to boys?!"

"Relax, Anna." She laughed. "Just be yourself. You talk to Danny fine."

"He doesn't really count."

"Yeah, I guess." Jess sighed, threw her arm around me, and led me to the first class of the day.

I arrived at detention in an extremely good mood that afternoon having had everyone be so nice about my new look all day.

Well, Mrs. Ginnwell did say that I looked a bit like a woman she once knew who these days lived in downtown

Chicago. She didn't expand. I wasn't quite sure if that was a positive comment or not, but since everyone else had been so nice, I hoped it might be.

I plonked myself down next to Connor. "Hey," he said sheepishly, breaking away from a conversation he was having with Max.

"Hey, how's it going?" I reached into my bag for my notebook. "How was your break?"

"Yeah, good." He looked awkward. "I was . . . um . . . were you okay and everything after the school trip?"

I blushed at the memory. "Yeah, I was fine. Sorry for being . . . rude."

"No, I'm sorry for . . . you know. Well, as long as you're okay."

"Yeah, I'm all good." I nodded. He nodded too and then for the first time since I'd got to know him, we didn't seem to know what to say to each other. I opened my textbook and tried to concentrate as Mr. Kenton sat at his desk, his head in his hands, poring over some essays and grumbling about teenagers' handwriting being "impossible to read nowadays."

I didn't last long.

"How's that new project coming along?" I asked Connor, nonchalantly turning a page in my textbook.

"It's still not ready."

I watched him as he studied a page in his sketchbook, making corrections.

"Don't you ever have homework to do?"

"Always." He grinned and looked up at me. "But I have my priorities."

When Mr. Kenton wearily got to his feet and announced it was time to go home, Connor watched me pack up and then blurted out, "Your hair is different."

"You just noticed?"

"No."

"Well, is it good different?"

"I guess . . ."

I must have looked insulted because he chuckled. "Relax, Spidey. It looks good. You look good."

"Oh." I felt my cheeks burning.

"Hey, Anna." Max walked by and whacked his bag at Connor's shoulder. My brain jerked into focus. "You like *Lord of the Rings* right?"

"Of course," I laughed, picking up the new book bag Mom had given me.

"There's a screening of the second movie in a couple of

weeks," Max said, looking at Connor who was staring at his feet.

"Oh right, the best one of the three," I said.

Max nodded slowly. "You just passed the test, oh young one."

I looked at him in anticipation.

Max took a deep breath and began to speak in a low, rumbling voice. "The world is indeed full of peril, and in it there are—"

"He's inviting you along," Connor interrupted before Max could go any further, standing and picking up his sketchbook. "There's a few of us going. Stop showing off, Max. It's not cool to know all the words."

"Yeah, that is just so not cool," I agreed, finishing the rest of the line in my head.

"Way to ruin a guy's moment." Max sighed. "Well, Anna, do you want to go? I can't promise I won't quote along with the film."

"He's being serious," Connor warned. "It will be fun though. You should come."

"Unless you have a premiere or something important to go to." Max grinned mischievously.

"Sounds good. I'll make sure I keep that night free of royal galas and celebrity parties," I teased, trying to act cool like

Jess always tells me but inwardly dancing around that I had received an invitation from someone who wasn't Jess, Danny, or Dog.

"How generous." Max laughed as we walked out of the room. "It's on the twenty-first of March."

"I'll put it in the calendar." I nodded. "Can Jess and Danny come too?"

"Course." Connor smiled, his eyes twinkling. "Everyone's welcome."

I was so excited that I immediately e-mailed Jess and Danny when I got home to tell them to keep that evening free so we could all go. They replied quickly to agree, and I felt like I might burst with happiness. Not only had I been invited to something, but I got to bring Jess and Danny along.

This whole change thing really was working out. I combed my bangs humming happily and then ran downstairs to do a victory dance with Dog.

Dad came barging out of his study angrily. "I can hardly hear myself think, Anna!" he moaned as I wobbled around the living room attempting to tango with Dog, who was actually impressively steady standing on his back legs. But not even Dad's temper could dampen the fact that I had been invited to watch a movie with a group of friends. ME. The person who never used to have anyone to sit next to on a bus.

But then disaster struck.

It was in the form of Sophie, who bounded over to me the next day with Josie. "Anna," she said, smiling and passing me an envelope. "Here, this is for you."

I opened it. "Wow, an invitation!" I cried in not a very cool way. I then coughed and said, "Cool," in a more casual manner as though I got invitations all the time.

Hello, I totally got an invitation yesterday. Check me out.

"It's my birthday. Friday the twenty-first." She grabbed Josie's hand and shook it excitedly. "It's going to be so fun. It's at my house. Dad's getting a DJ and everything."

My face dropped. "The twenty-first? Of March?"

"Yeah, it says there." She pointed at the pink invite and then looked up, frowning. "Can't you come?"

"You're not too busy at a premiere or a celebrity party that night or something?" Josie added, looking at Sophie pointedly.

I swallowed. I had already accepted the invite to the *Lord of the Rings* screening and asked Jess and Danny to go. I'd told Connor I'd be there.

But could I turn down an invitation to what was probably

going to be the most exciting birthday party of our class? This was what I had done everything for—and it was working.

Then, out of nowhere, Brendan Dakers was suddenly looking over my shoulder at the invite in my hand. "It's going to be so cool, Soph," he said, standing so close behind me that the hair on the back of my neck stood on end.

"I know; I just gave Anna her invitation." Sophie leaned into him.

Josie smirked, folding her arms and watching me.

"Good stuff," Brendan said. "You are coming, right, Anna?"

"Uh," I replied, opening my locker door and groaning inwardly as my history textbook toppled out and slammed onto the floor. I bent down to pick it up clumsily, and as I stood straight, struggling to balance it on top of my other books, Brendan reached out. He took the history book and carefully arranged it back in my locker.

"Wouldn't be right without our very own It Girl there," he said, winking.

"So," Sophie prompted, coming around the other side of Brendan so she was back in front of me, "can you come?"

I looked up. Brendan smiled at me.

"Of course I can come." I nodded confidently. "I'll be there."

From: rebecca.blythe@bouncemail.co.uk
To: anna_huntley@zingmail.co.uk
Cc: marianne@montaines.co.uk;
helena@montaines.co.uk
Subject: Re: Confused
Darling, I hope you don't mind–I've copied Helena and Marianne on your e-mail, because I thought they might also be able to help.
I think it's wonderful that you've been invited to a party! You must go. You're only young once.
I see your dilemma though. In my experience, honesty is the best policy. Explain to the others that you can go to a screening with them another time but you've been invited to a friend's birthday party that you feel you should attend.
Unless you're not close to this girl who is throwing the party?
Mom xxx

From: helena@montaines.co.uk
To: rebecca.blythe@bouncemail.co.uk
Cc: anna_huntley@zingmail.co.uk; marianne@montaines.co.uk
Subject: Re: Confused

I remember having a very similar problem when Prince Michael of Kent invited me to a black tie ball the same night I had a date with George Clooney.

I picked the date because George would have been very distressed otherwise and I'd just had an eyebrow wax that day.

Helena x

From: marianne@montaines.co.uk
To: helena@montaines.co.uk
Cc: anna_huntley@zingmail.co.uk; rebecca.blythe@bouncemail.co.uk
Subject: Re: Confused

Mom. That was the worst advice ever. It wasn't even advice. And it was WAY too much information. Please keep your hair removal details to yourself.

Anna, do what you feel is right. If you think that Jess and your friends will be very let down, then maybe the right thing to do is to go to the screening?
But, like your mom pointed out, screenings happen often. Birthdays are only once a year. Go with your gut.
Marianne x

From: rebecca.blythe@bouncemail.co.uk
To: marianne@montaines.co.uk
Cc: anna_huntley@zingmail.co.uk; helena@montaines.co.uk
Subject: By the way
Just out of interest, who is this Connor fellow?
Rebecca xxx

From: marianne@montaines.co.uk
To: rebecca.blythe@bouncemail.co.uk
Cc: anna_huntley@zingmail.co.uk; helena@montaines.co.uk
Subject: Re: By the way
Yeah, he hasn't come up before, and now

suddenly you've mentioned him a couple of times?

Marianne x

From: helena@montaines.co.uk

To: marianne@montaines.co.uk

Cc: anna_huntley@zingmail.co.uk;

rebecca.blythe@bouncemail.co.uk

Subject: Re: By the way

Oh how lovely! Is Connor your new beau?

Helena x

From: marianne@montaines.co.uk

To: helena@montaines.co.uk

Cc: anna_huntley@zingmail.co.uk;

rebecca.blythe@bouncemail.co.uk

Subject: Re: By the way

MOM. Please don't use the expression "beau." It last got used in the sixteenth century by people wearing big wigs and too much powder.

Marianne x

From: helena@montaines.co.uk

To: marianne@montaines.co.uk

in South Africa. I was actually rather talented. Perhaps you'd like me to teach you some?

From: helena@montaines.co.uk
To: rebecca.blythe@bouncemail.co.uk
Cc: anna_huntley@zingmail.co.uk; marianne@montaines.co.uk
Subject: Re: More confused

Oh was that your Boursin? I had some the other day, I do apologize. It was in Nick's fridge and so I put it in the salad. Were you saving it?
Helena x
PS That would be wonderful! I bet you're a great rapper, Rebecca. You could give me lessons!

From: marianne@montaines.co.uk
To: helena@montaines.co.uk
Cc: anna_huntley@zingmail.co.uk; rebecca.blythe@bouncemail.co.uk
Subject: Re: More confused

Please, neither of you ever rap in public. That's all I ask.
Anna, is Connor into music? Maybe you can

KA

Cc: anna_huntley@zingmail.co.uk;
rebecca.blythe@bouncemail.co.uk
Subject: Re: By the way

That is not true. It has been used in this by rappers in dreadful rap songs. I kno thanks to you, darling daughter, blaring garbage at all hours.

If you ask me, she should spend less tim rapping terribly about him and more tim ing him happy. Then her "beau" might pa more attention and we wouldn't have to l to her woes through the medium of rap c radio.

Helena x

From: rebecca.blythe@bouncemail.co.ul
To: helena@montaines.co.uk
Cc: anna_huntley@zingmail.co.uk;
marianne@montaines.co.uk
Subject: More confused

Anna, what happened to Boursin?

Rebecca xxx

PS Helena, I tried rapping once when I

ask him to On the Rox to make up for ditching him at the screening?
If he's into you, then he won't care if you cancel the screening and ask him to a show instead.
Way more fun.
Marianne x

From: helena@montaines.co.uk
To: marianne@montaines.co.uk
Cc: anna_huntley@zingmail.co.uk;
rebecca.blythe@bouncemail.co.uk
Subject: Re: More confused
My God, Marianne, is that how you treat men?
Ditch them when they invite you to nice, romantic screenings and then lure them to immoral rock shows instead?
As soon as you come back from this jaunt in Barcelona we are sitting down and having a talk, young lady.
Helena x

From: marianne@montaines.co.uk
To: helena@montaines.co.uk

Cc: anna_huntley@zingmail.co.uk;
rebecca.blythe@bouncemail.co.uk
Subject: What is wrong with you?
Mom, in case you had forgotten, you MARRIED a rock musician. That's how I came about. So don't give me heat about "immoral" shows thank you very much.
And I would hardly call *Lord of the Rings* romantic. That Yoda dude doesn't exactly set the mood.
Marianne x

From: rebecca.blythe@bouncemail.co.uk
To: marianne@montaines.co.uk
Cc: anna_huntley@zingmail.co.uk;
helena@montaines.co.uk
Subject: Re: What is wrong with you?
No, my love, Yoda is in *Star Trek*, not *Lord of the Rings*.
Rebecca x

From: marianne@montaines.co.uk
To: rebecca.blythe@bouncemail.co.uk

Cc: anna_huntley@zingmail.co.uk;
helena@montaines.co.uk
Subject: Re: What is wrong with you?
Whatever. They're both basically the same thing, right?
Marianne x

From: helena@montaines.co.uk
To: marianne@montaines.co.uk
Cc: anna_huntley@zingmail.co.uk;
rebecca.blythe@bouncemail.co.uk
Subject: Re: What is wrong with you?
I actually auditioned for *Star Trek* once.
I didn't get the part because they said I looked too young.
Helena x

From: marianne@montaines.co.uk
To: helena@montaines.co.uk
Cc: anna_huntley@zingmail.co.uk;
rebecca.blythe@bouncemail.co.uk
Subject: Sure
Stop lying to yourself, Mom. You didn't get the

part because you did it in a Jamaican accent.
Marianne x

From: rebecca.blythe@bouncemail.co.uk
To: marianne@montaines.co.uk
Cc: anna_huntley@zingmail.co.uk; helena@montaines.co.uk
Subject: Re: Sure
I'm sure your audition was wonderful, Helena. I personally think most action films could be brought up a notch if they threw in more Jamaican accents.
Anna darling, if you're struggling with your feelings about Connor and Boursin, maybe you need to take a step back from both of them and think about what you want.
Rebecca xxx

From: helena@montaines.co.uk
To: rebecca.blythe@bouncemail.co.uk
Cc: anna_huntley@zingmail.co.uk; marianne@montaines.co.uk
Subject: Re: Sure

Thank you, Rebecca, you are kind. The part went to someone who had a botched nose job and eventually had an affair with one of those monkey actors from *Planet of the Apes* so I wasn't that upset.

I agree with your mother, Anna, you need to think carefully. Ask yourself, who would you rather spend your time with? Connor or Boursin?

Once you've worked that out, you'll know what to do.

Helena x

From: marianne@montaines.co.uk

To: helena@montaines.co.uk

Cc: anna_huntley@zingmail.co.uk; rebecca.blythe@bouncemail.co.uk

Subject: Re: Sure

I'm confused. Are we talking about men or food?

Marianne x

From: anna_huntley@zingmail.co.uk

To: marianne@montaines.co.uk

Cc: rebecca.blythe@gmail.com; helena@montaines.co.uk
Subject: STOP THIS AT ONCE

First things first, Yoda is in *STAR WARS*. Not *Star Trek*. I'm ashamed of all of you.

Secondly, Mom, how many times do I need to tell you this . . . Boursin is a CHEESE. His name is Brendan. Seriously, it's not that out there. B-R-E-N-D-A-N.

Thirdly, I am not "struggling" with my feelings for Brendan . . . or Connor for that matter. Seriously, we are just friends. And anyway, I only ever really see him in detention. That's pretty much it. So yeah, we're just FRIENDS. So drop that one please because it is so not how it is.

Lastly, I want you all to know that you have managed to confuse me EVEN MORE than I already was.

Now, if you'll excuse me, I'm going to go and eat some Nutella. I have already consumed an entire bag of strawberry truffles. Do you see the state you have driven me to?!

Love, me xxx

From: rebecca.blythe@bouncemail.co.uk

To: helena@montaines.co.uk

Subject: Anna's e-mail

I don't know about you, but I'm sure grateful not to be twelve years old.

Aren't you?

Rebecca xxx

19.

So you're sure you're not mad about the screening thing? Sorry to bring it up again.

Anna, why would I be mad? Of course I'm not mad.

I feel really bad about it. I wish they weren't on the same day.

Yeah.

You and Danny should come to the party. And Connor.

Ha. We didn't get invites.

Well, I don't think that matters. Maybe she hasn't finished giving them out.

Honestly, Anna, don't worry about it. You'll have fun at the party.

So would you if you came.

I'd rather go to the screening. Danny would too. It'll be nice to hang out with Connor and those guys—I don't know them very well.

Oh, okay.

I saw you in the papers this morning. Mom showed me. Your dress was amazing. You didn't tell me you were going to a ball.

Oh that. Yeah, it was a last-minute thing that Helena and Marianne invited me to. The dress was Prada. Me... in Prada! Can you believe that?!

Wow. It was very pretty. You looked great.

I steered clear of soy sauce that's for sure. It's so weird. People have started sending me stuff this week. Designers, I mean. It's really cool. I got sent this jacket that I definitely couldn't wear but I think you will love it. You want to come over after school and try it on?

Thanks! By the way, have you asked Marianne or Helena about any photographers I can talk to? I don't mind what sort of photography they do, it can be anything!

Haven't had a chance to ask them. Promise I will.

Okay, thanks. You and Brendan have been talking a lot this week. He seems to aim all his conversations at you during lunch.

Do you think?! It's amazing, isn't it? We just get along really well I guess, although I'm still not very good at talking to him. I know this sounds crazy, Jess, but I have noticed him paying me more attention.

Yeah, we all have.

Do you think it's CRAZY of me to think that there

might be a chance of him asking me to the Beatus dance? I know it's ridiculous but the other day he did ask if I had bought a dress for it yet.

Did he?

Yeah! I said that I hadn't because I didn't have a date yet and then he smiled. HE SMILED. What do you think that means?!

I don't know. Maybe he is thinking of asking you.

ARGH! CAN YOU IMAGINE?!

It would be pretty insane. Are you sure that's what you want?

Of course I'm sure! Why wouldn't I be? It would be GREAT. Jess, the most popular boy in school likes us! This stuff never happens. Isn't this better than before?

The most popular boy in school likes you, not us.

I think he puts up with me and Danny. Sophie and Josie make that pretty clear. What do you mean about before?

That's not true! You're much more interesting than I am. They're getting to know us, that's all.

Maybe. The getting to know us bit, that is.

I'd better tell Connor and Max in detention today that I can't go anymore. I keep putting it off. Do you think they'll be mad?

No, Anna, I don't think so. They'll get it, like Danny and I do.

Get what?

The It Girl thing. Better stop passing notes. Ms. Brockley is looking this way.

I wasn't sure if Connor did get it. When I told him he seemed annoyed and almost baffled.

"Sophie *Parker*?" he sort of sneered as though he wasn't sure if I was joking or not.

"Yeah, I know. I wish it was on another night, but it is her birthday. She can't really switch that." I laughed nervously, attempting to lighten the mood, because the way Connor was suddenly looking at me made me feel very tense.

"But . . . you love *Lord of the Rings*. You really want to go to Sophie Parker's birthday party? Seriously?"

"Of course I do, she's my friend! Like I said to Max, I'll definitely be there the next time a screening happens. And I can see if maybe you guys can come to her party too or something . . ." I trailed off as we both knew that wasn't an option. Not when it came to Connor.

"That's okay, thanks. I'll pass. So, are Jess and Danny still coming to the movie?"

"Yeah." I nodded, feeling a little deflated. "Yeah, they're still going."

He studied my face and then shook his head.

"What?"

"I just . . ." He looked at me and then sighed and turned back to his work. "Nothing."

"No, what were you going to say?" I encouraged.

"Nothing, Anna, don't worry about it," he snapped.

I don't know why he had to make me feel so guilty when everyone else had been so nice about it. His mood didn't improve with me as the night of Sophie's party drew near. I tried to ask him about his drawings, but he didn't seem to want to talk to me. I even made a comment one day about Gwen Stacy being Spider-Man's one true love rather than Mary Jane, and he barely flinched.

Connor not talking to me made me feel weird.

But the night of Sophie's party I knew I had made the right decision. So many people were going who I wanted to talk to. If someone as popular as Sophie invites you to a party, then you know that you're doing the right thing. Going to Sophie's party and looking like an It Girl meant that I could make friends with people in my grade who never used to talk to me, and if they liked me, then they would start inviting Jess and Danny to things too. Maybe even Connor would come around. Then all of us could hang out together, and there wouldn't be this weird divide.

It made complete sense.

Connor was just being stubborn, I thought to myself as I hunted around my bedroom for my shoe before the party. Maybe if I explained, he would start being himself around me again.

Suddenly my dad yelled up the stairs that we had to get going, and I had to put my thoughts about Connor aside and finish looking for my shoe, which turned out to be lying on top of the silverware in the dishwasher because on the rare occasion that Dad haphazardly leaves it open Dog likes to keep things safe in there.

I picked out another pair of shoes and we set off.

Of course, my dad tried to embarrass me as much as possible. He insisted on coming into Sophie's house with me and hunting down her parents to say hello and to tell them he would be picking me up at eleven o'clock sharp. I cringed as Sophie and Josie stood nearby whispering to each other.

"Happy birthday, Sophie," my dad said to her when he forced me to introduce them.

"Thank you, Mr. Huntley." She giggled. "Congratulations on your engagement. If you and Helena want to come join us at the end of the party, my parents would be more than happy."

"That's very kind, but I'm actually working on a very interesting chapter in my book about gas masks."

It couldn't have been a celebrity party or something cool keeping you from a drink with Sophie's parents, could it, Dad. It HAD to be a chapter on gas masks.

"It's actually very fascinating," Dad began, and I saw Sophie's fixed smile wobble.

"Okay thanks, bye, Dad!" I interrupted, basically pushing him out the door. I made my way back to Sophie and Josie and laughed nervously. "Parents, huh."

"Yeah," Sophie agreed. "You look nice. I like your jacket."

"Thanks!" I said, brushing the leather sleeve. "I'm going to give it to Jess after this."

"Really?" Josie snorted. "I think it's better for you."

Sophie smiled. "I'll see you later. Have fun."

As the pair floated away to greet other guests, I felt uncomfortable and wasn't sure why. I was at the most popular party of the year—and things were getting better already at school; I just needed to embrace it. I tried not to think about Jess and Danny at the screening with Connor—the movie would have started by now. I bet they were all getting along really well. It made sense. Connor would love the fact that Jess was into *Lord of the Rings.*

I pushed aside the sinking feeling in my stomach as Brendan came over. "Hey, It Girl," he said, pushing his bangs out of his eyes. "Nice jacket."

"Yeah, it's a hit." I smiled back weakly.

"I've been meaning to talk to you." He grabbed my hand

and pulled me over to sit on some cushions and rugs that had been laid out in the garden. My stomach flipped in excitement. "I saw that Marianne was on a date with the lead singer of On the Rox. It was in the papers this week."

"Yeah." I nodded.

"That's crazy. They're my favorite band!"

"Really? No way," I said, noticing that our knees were touching. I suddenly felt very hot. "I'm actually going to see them next week. Marianne got me tickets."

"That is so cool!" He leaned in so that our faces were almost touching. "Promise to tell me all about it?"

"I . . . uh . . . yeah." Since it was obvious I had nothing else intelligent to say, Brendan smiled and got up, ready to walk away.

My mouth went dry. "You should come," I blurted out suddenly, unable to tear my gaze from him.

"You serious?" He sat down, grabbed my hand, and squeezed it. "That would be incredible! Thanks, Anna."

I was about to respond when Josie and Sophie slumped down next to us. Brendan dropped my hand quickly. Surprised by the sudden change, my brain kicked in again, and I realized that I had just asked Brendan to the show I had promised to take Jess to.

"I've been meaning to ask you," I said quickly to them, hoping Brendan wouldn't say anything about the show. "How are things looking for the Beatus dance?"

"Oh my goodness, it's going to be the best." Sophie nodded, glancing at Brendan. "The most exciting thing will be the announcement of the raffle of course. It was so kind of your mom to offer the prize, Brendan. We've raised plenty of money, so the dance will look really great."

Brendan shrugged. "No sweat."

"Well, I know that I would be so excited if I won," Sophie said, giving him a big smile. "I would love to learn from someone as successful as your mom."

I reminded myself that Sophie had said at the park that she didn't like Brendan and tried to enjoy the rest of the party.

I was pleased though when my dad pulled up outside the house as promised at eleven o'clock. I smiled as I saw Dog hanging out of the back, his paws resting on the window ledge and his head sticking out.

"Hey, Anna!" I turned around and Brendan was coming toward me. "Thanks again about the show."

"Oh that." I gulped. "Yeah, cool. Maybe don't tell anyone until I definitely have the tickets. Let's keep it between us?"

"Sure," he said, but he seemed distracted. "So . . . um,

do . . . you . . . have a date to the Beatus dance?" He shuffled his feet.

I looked up at him. "No," I pretty much whispered back. He smiled, as though relieved.

"Anna!" my dad called from behind me as he beeped the horn. "Come on, I need to get home quickly. I just had an idea about gas!"

Brendan's eyes widened.

"Gas masks," I said quickly by way of explanation. "He's writing a chapter for a book on gas masks. Not just . . . gas."

"Right. Cool." Brendan shrugged. "See you at school then."

He shoved his hands in his pockets, grinned at me, and made his way back into the house. I stood in shock for a few more seconds until Dad started beeping his horn again.

I climbed in the car and Dog immediately attacked, slobbering all over my jacket.

"A good evening?" Dad asked politely, not really listening and clearly still distracted by gas thoughts.

"An interesting one," I replied with a sigh.

How on earth were things so good—I really thought Brendan was going to ask me to the dance—but so bad at the same time? I had offered him tickets that I'd already promised to Jess.

My head hurt.

I AM A TERRIBLE LIAR, SO I DON'T LIE VERY OFTEN.

Not because I'm a good person. If I could get away with it, I bet I would lie all the time. But something in my face gives me away. Dad says it's because my eyes go really wide and I don't blink the whole time I'm speaking. Apparently it's very creepy and puts him on edge.

The main lies I have told in my life are as follows:

1. Every year I lie about something to get out of sports day. *I try to make it different each year, you know, just to make it more believable. Sometimes I want the lie so badly that it actually becomes the truth. Like the time I lied about feeling very sick, and then I got so worked up that Dad was going to call the doctor and I would get discovered that I projectile*

vomited all over Dad when he had the audacity to ask me if I was trying to get out of going to sports day.

2. That it wasn't me who hid Dad's manuscript behind the radiator that ended up catching fire. *This sounds bad to admit because I set Josie Graham on fire, but I SWEAR I am not a pyromaniac. It's just that I'd spilled my grape soda all over Dad's manuscript, and he was going for a meeting with his editor that day so I knew he needed it. I panicked and threw it down by the radiator. He thought he'd lost it somehow, and then later that day when he was in his meeting, making excuses about turning up without a manuscript, the babysitter and I were busy running around trying to save things in his study that had turned into a giant furnace.*

3. When I told Mom that Dad had gone to a cooking class. *This was a necessary lie. I knew that Mom had always felt guilty about traveling all the time leaving Dad to raise me. I thought that if she believed Dad had improved his cooking skills, she might feel better about everything.*

I still haven't told her that this never took place and have to be on my toes every time she comes to stay. When she asks Dad how he has no idea how to use a whisk when he went to the most expensive cooking class in London, I have to jump in there with a change of conversation that will distract her. This lie also means that we have to constantly eat out while she stays, but it has to look like a natural decision. I have become very good at this over the years.

4. When I lied to Jess about not having tickets to the On the Rox show. *This is the worst lie I've told.*

She didn't even look that mad. She just looked disappointed. "Oh, that's okay, Anna."

"Marianne thought she had enough tickets, but it turns out she doesn't."

"Right, well, you can't do anything about that." Jess shrugged. She smiled at me when she saw my facial expression. "Anna, it's not a big deal; don't worry about it."

It was a big deal, because I knew that she had really wanted to see them; she had been looking forward to it for weeks. I had asked Marianne if there was any chance of getting another ticket, but they were all sold out and there were no backstage passes left. I searched Jess's expression.

"We can see them another time. I don't think they're touring for a bit, but next time they come to London we can go." She offered me a gummy bear. I declined. "You'd like them. It's a shame that you can't go either. Who is Marianne taking?"

"Some friends I think." My heart sank at how kind Jess was being.

"Well, that's fair enough. It was nice of her to offer though. Never mind."

"Maybe we can go to another show? Is there another band you like?" I asked desperately.

"Of course. On the Rox are my favorite, but I like lots of bands." She nodded optimistically. "I'm sure you'll get invited to some more."

"Yeah," I agreed, downhearted.

"Please don't get upset, Anna; honestly, it's not your fault." She picked up her bag. "Anyway, the show is right before the Beatus dance, isn't it? This way we can have a relaxing week before the dance."

"You're definitely going to the Beatus?" I asked, momentarily distracted.

"Yes." Jess lifted her eyes to the ceiling. "Has Brendan asked you yet?"

"Brendan? Why would Brendan ask me?"

"I don't know, genius." She chuckled. "Maybe because you've wanted that ever since you heard about the Beatus dance and the past few weeks you two have become quite close?"

"Oh, ha no. He hasn't asked me. Has anyone asked you?"

Jess snorted. "No, not yet."

"Not yet?"

"Well, there's still a few days, Anna; you never know what might happen. Hey, what's wrong? I'm just joking. I'll be going with Danny like we agreed. You look upset."

I wondered if Jess really had been joking. Or did she think someone other than Danny might ask her to the dance? Maybe the screening had gone much better than I'd imagined. . . .

As I got home, I was hit by the overwhelming feeling of wanting to cry. I could hear Dad on the phone in his study, so I grabbed Dog's collar and took him with me into the closet. I wanted to cuddle into Dog's fur, but it became apparent, as soon as I shut the closet door and Dog and I were alone in a confined space, that Dog had rolled in something that day.

As I was chastising him for being smelly, he heard Dad make a sound in the hall, so he tugged free of my grip and barged out of the closet and into the hall, where he proceeded to attack a plug.

"Anna, are you in there?" I heard Dad scramble around the telephone table, and then he was standing in the doorway peering in. "What's wrong?"

"Nothing," I whimpered.

"You look upset."

"I'm not upset," I responded, hoping the darkness wouldn't give away my red, blotchy face.

"Will you come out here and talk about it?"

"I like it in here."

Dad paused for a moment and then crouched down and crawled into the closet and shut the door so we were in complete darkness.

"Dad, what are you doing?"

"I thought you might find it easier to talk to me in here."

"You must be busy. You've got that gas chapter."

"It can wait. You want to talk about it? You don't have to. We can sit in here in silence for a bit, and then I could order you Chinese food for when you're ready to come out?" I heard him shuffle as he got comfortable. I felt big in the closet, so it can't have been very comfortable for him.

"I haven't been very nice."

"Well, that can't be right."

"I haven't. Marianne offered me tickets to a show, so I invited Jess to come with me. But then there's this guy . . ."

Dad waited a moment and then spoke when it was clear I was faltering. "Go on."

"Dad. You can't be weird."

"I'm not being weird."

"You're always being weird."

"*You're* always being weird."

"And whose fault is that?" I argued. "Fine. You can't be weird when I talk about boys."

He sighed. "Okay, I promise I won't be weird when we talk about boys."

I eyed him up suspiciously in spite of not really being able to see him, but I did it for effect anyway and then took a deep breath. "There's this boy who I think likes me. He happens to be the most perfect, amazing, popular boy in school. And he likes *me*. I think he does anyway." I paused, trying to work out how to put it in a way that old people might understand.

"Go on," Dad encouraged.

"Well I want him to invite me to the dance next week. Because then I would be popular and normal too. And everyone would be happy. So I invited him to the show."

"The same show you invited Jess to?"

"Yes. So then I had to tell her I didn't have tickets anymore. Because I didn't want to hurt her by telling her I'd invited Brendan instead. She looked so sad when I said we couldn't go anymore."

I paused again. My dad cleared his throat. "All right, go on."

"I've told Brendan not to brag about it. I don't want Jess finding out. But she was so nice about it and I was lying to her. It was horrible."

"I see." Dad waited patiently for more. I didn't say anything. "Anna. Considering we're sitting in a closet, I'm going to guess that taking Brendan to the show isn't actually what you want to do."

I sighed. "I don't know. I think somehow I might actually have a chance with Brendan. If I don't invite him to the show, he might not invite me to the dance."

"If Brendan really likes you," Dad said gently, reaching out for my foot, which he grabbed and shook, "he will ask you to the dance whether you take him or Jess to the show. Don't you think?"

"Um . . ."

"Anna. Boys don't just like girls because they invite them

to things. You promised these tickets to Jess. Brendan will understand."

"You're right. What do I do?"

"Simple. Tell Brendan you promised the ticket to Jess first. That you'll take him to the next one. He might be disappointed, but Jess has been a very good friend to you. Especially during the chaos of my engagement." He chuckled. "I haven't heard of Brendan until recently. Or that other boy you keep mentioning, Conway or something."

"I'm not sure he's my biggest fan either."

"You'll sort it out just by talking to them. And if you can't, then you can always invite them along to something fun like an air show. Oh, there's a great talk coming up actually, given by an expert in land mines. I can always try to rustle up some tickets . . . they'll love that!"

"I'll talk to them I think, thanks, Dad," I said hurriedly. "We can leave the closet now."

"Excellent news. Glad I could help. I'm getting a leg cramp."

After we had crawled out of the closet and Dad had awkwardly pulled me in for a big hug, which Dog had then tried to gate-crash, I decided to take Dog for a walk in the hope of finding Brendan playing soccer in the park so I could explain to him that I would be taking Jess to On the Rox.

Instead of Brendan and the boys, I spotted Josie with a couple of the girls from our class, Debbie and Scarlet, with their backs toward me, sitting cross-legged on one of the benches, reading magazines. It was strange to see Josie without Sophie, but I figured that Sophie was probably at a sports practice and Josie had to make do with others until her return.

I made my way toward them to say hi, dragging Dog with me, who was growling at a squirrel nearby. As I got closer, I overheard them talking and slowed when I heard my name.

"Oh my goodness, look at Anna here." Josie was sniggering, pointing at a page. "This should be in the worst-dressed column surely. They must have made a mistake. She needs a stylist."

"Well, it's not like she has the best guidance." Debbie raised her eyebrows. "Marianne Montaine is usually a fashion disaster. I would die of embarrassment if I had to be associated with someone like her."

"Hello? She has to be associated with Anna. Hardly a dream come true for a celebrity. At least she's figured out her hair. It's *something*." Josie sighed. "It's embarrassing though that she thinks that she's . . . I don't know . . ."

"Important?" Scarlet suggested.

"No, not that. Until this whole It Girl thing happened, she was a loser. You can't just change overnight. The only thing that's different is her dad's marital status," she snorted.

"Brendan likes her," Debbie pointed out, flicking the page of the magazine.

"Not really," Josie scoffed. "He puts up with her probably. He wouldn't actually think of hanging out with her for real. Like one on one."

"I heard that he might ask her out. Maybe to the Beatus dance," Debbie said authoritatively.

"Who told you that?" Josie laughed. "Don't be silly. I'm sure that Brendan thinks the same as I do. Anna is a loser. And once a loser, always a loser." Josie smugly took the magazine from Debbie and flicked to the fashion page.

I felt tears of hurt and anger running down my cheeks as they giggled together. Dog started a low growl and I ran with him on the leash, praying that they didn't see me.

As I came around the corner to our house, Danny appeared. "Hey, Anna, I was just at your house. Your dad said you were out for a walk. I wanted to return all those DVDs you lent me. They were great—I was just discussing them with your dad." He noticed my face as I looked up at him. "Hey, what's wrong? Have you been crying?"

"No," I said, determinedly wiping my cheeks.

"Look, if this is about Jess," he said, looking confused, "she's not mad at you, Anna. It's not your fault that you don't have the tickets anymore."

"Danny." I was exhausted. "Everyone thinks I'm the biggest loser in the world. I have to prove to them I'm not."

"What? I don't think you're the biggest loser in the world." He frowned. "I think you're very cool."

"You think I'm cool?"

"Yeah! I mean, not in the same way Sophie Parker is." He rolled his eyes. "I know you really like her but she's fake. You're cool in a different way. You're interesting and funny. You're really odd." I smiled and he continued. "Odd in a good way though. I think it's cool that you know loads about movies that I haven't heard of. And you read cool books and stuff. Plus you're really nice." He shrugged. "Yeah, I think you're cool."

"Thanks, Danny."

That night, I lay in my dog pajamas and wondered whether everyone else at school except Jess and Danny felt the same way Josie did. Had they all been laughing at me, all along? Poor Anna, they must have been saying all this time, thinking she's popular when she's not. How mortifying that they had all been making fun of me when I wasn't there, maybe even making fun of me to my face without me realizing.

I grew hot with anger and threw my covers off. I had to prove everyone wrong. If Brendan went to the show with me, then he would definitely ask me to the dance after that. Then they wouldn't think I was a loser anymore.

Jess would understand. She would probably encourage me to take Brendan. I was embarrassed that I had drawn attention to her and Danny yet again. Josie and her friends must have been laughing at them behind their backs too. I wasn't going to let that continue.

From: dantheman@zingmail.co.uk
To: anna_huntley@zingmail.co.uk
Subject: Today

Hi, Anna,

Just wanted to check that you were definitely okay today? I hope you know that you can talk to me and Jess anytime you need. You seemed very quiet when we walked back to your house.

I thought of another reason why you're not a loser:

you don't pretend to be someone you're not.
That's really cool.
Don't tell anyone I said something like that–it's pretty embarrassing and won't do anything for my street cred. Not that I have street cred. But just in case I do.
All right. Bye.
Danny

21.

EIGHT THINGS THAT I HAVE BEEN VERY WRONG about:

1. You could only be a princess if you had long hair.
2. Pepto-Bismol would taste just like a strawberry milkshake.
3. Buying black corduroy bell-bottoms was a good idea.
4. If Dog loved dog biscuits so much, they couldn't taste so bad.
5. I could read a map. In France. When Dad was driving.
6. That becoming a Jedi was a viable option.
7. Andy Murray's level of emotion. The 2012 Wimbledon final loss to Federer was a game changer.

8. Wanting Brendan Dakers to take me to the Beatus dance.

I should have known the moment we showed up at the show. Marianne had given us strict instructions to meet her by the stage door around the back of the building as there was no way she was going in the normal entrance. "The press will know I'm going," she had said, sighing on the phone to me the night before. "They won't leave me alone."

So I had agreed to meet Brendan at eight o'clock at the venue and, when he arrived, I directed him to the back of the building. As we stood there waiting for someone to tell us what to do, Brendan started going on about how excited he was to be there. "I bet there's going to be some cool people inside."

"Maybe," I said, pulling nervously at the leather jacket he had said looked nice on me at Sophie's party.

"I haven't met many famous people."

"Your mom must be around famous people all the time. Supermodels on fashion shoots, actors she's photographing?"

"Yeah but I never get to meet them." He kicked a pebble that went skittering across the road. "She never lets me come to photo shoots."

"Oh right."

He kicked another pebble.

"I feel like I probably should have listened to On the Rox a lot more before tonight," I joked.

"Yeah?"

"Yeah, I won't know many words. I'm more of a movie person than a music person I think."

"Oh right." He smiled at me. "That's cool."

"You like movies?"

"Yeah, movies are cool."

"I like superhero movies."

How was it that I was getting WORSE at talking to boys?

"Yeah. The Wolverine thermal underwear, right?"

KILL ME NOW.

"Ha, yeah. Right."

Thankfully, we were both rescued from the most awkward conversation of all time because the stage door opened, and a large man with a bald head and an earpiece ushered us in.

"Follow the hallway down and through the next door. They'll figure out your backstage passes."

Seriously, why are all bouncers bald? Is it a requirement of that line of work? I made a note to myself to google it later.

"Backstage passes?" Brendan asked, looking straight ahead as we walked down the hall. "Cool."

Marianne greeted us on the other side of the door, looking surprised at Brendan. "I thought . . ."

"This is Brendan," I said quickly, hoping she wouldn't make a big deal about Jess not being there.

"Right. Nice to meet you."

"You too." Brendan shook her hand, staring in awe.

"You a fan of On the Rox, Brendan?"

"Yeah, I really love them."

"Have you even listened to them, Anna?" she teased.

"I have one hundred percent listened to them and they are GREAT."

"Can you name one of their songs?"

"Please," I scoffed. "I am not going to rise to this."

"So that's a no." She laughed. "I hope your knowledge is better than hers, Brendan."

"It *definitely* is," he replied a little too enthusiastically.

"Let's go through," Marianne instructed. "I think it's about to start. What drinks do you guys want? Lemonade or something?"

"Yes please." I nodded.

"Same," Brendan said. "I'll help you carry them."

"That's okay, you go on and I'll come join you guys. Just stay on this side and don't go too far into the crowd. It's busy and I'll never find you—especially since you don't have your phone, Anna."

Dog had helpfully stored my phone in the toilet bowl for safekeeping that morning. It meant that we had to stick rigidly to any meeting plans, but to tell the truth, I was enjoying the freedom from Dad checking up to see that I hadn't run off with someone from a boy band every ten minutes.

I followed Brendan through the doors and suddenly felt nervous as I realized it was just the two of us. I wasn't sure why. Maybe it was just strange being alone with Brendan. Usually we were surrounded by everyone else, so now that it was just me and the most popular boy in school, I really felt the pressure to say and do the right thing.

Or maybe I was just feeling uncomfortable because the thermal underwear had been brought up. The mere memory of it was enough to ruin a perfectly pleasant evening.

The main room was packed full of teenagers. Brendan and I did as we'd agreed and hung back away from the crowd so that Marianne would be able to find us. Brendan craned his neck over the mass. "Wow, this is really cool," he said, looking around him. "Thanks for bringing me, Anna."

"No problem." I smiled.

"I think they might start soon."

"Yeah, they're due on any minute."

"Let's get closer," he said, turning to me excitedly.

"Yeah, definitely, but let's wait for Marianne first."

"She might take forever at the bar; come on." He grabbed my hand and I blushed. It felt nice.

"I don't know—she might not be able to find us. I'd rather wait."

He looked at me and then let go of my hand, obviously disappointed. "Okay."

"We can go up to the front in a minute, as soon as she's back."

"Yeah." He nodded, watching as everyone crowded together toward the front. "Might be too packed in a minute."

I felt even more uncomfortable than before. Why couldn't I just have done what he asked and gone with him to the front? It was Brendan Dakers! Girls in my grade would do anything to go with him to a show and have him take their hand and lead them to the front of the stage. I tried to think of something to say to make up for it, but my brain just couldn't work fast enough. He made me too nervous.

"There you are." Marianne came up behind us, holding out the drinks. "It's so hard to make out who is who in here."

"Thanks." Brendan smiled as he took his drink from her.

"No worries. I think they're going on in a minute. Tom said they wouldn't be long."

"Whoa, are you talking about the lead singer, Tom Kyzer?" Brendan's eyes widened.

"Yeah, I was with him earlier backstage. It's so weird, he still gets nervous, even though he's performed hundreds of times."

"Really?" I asked. "That's kind of comforting to know that rock stars still get nervous. Does he have any cool rituals before he goes on stage? Like tennis players do before they play?"

Before she could answer, Brendan cut in. "Do you think we might be able to use our backstage passes too and go with you to meet the band? Later on, after the show?"

"Maybe." Marianne shrugged. "It depends on the time. We can't get back too late. Your parents would kill me."

"Mine don't care," Brendan hastily assured her. "It would be pretty cool if you introduced us."

"Well, if we have time," Marianne said, looking at me.

The lights suddenly flared up on the stage, and the band emerged to an eruption of screams from the crowd. Marianne and I started laughing at all the people at the front of the standing area, jumping up and down and reaching outward desperately toward the band. "That's why you want to be a rock star," Marianne yelled over the noise. "Imagine the feeling you would get."

"You would feel so awesome," Brendan shouted back.

They struck up the first song, and the three of us just stood there, bopping along as the rest of the audience went crazy.

"I think we should go to the front," Brendan said after a few minutes. "That's where all the action is."

"I'm not a fan of all that," Marianne admitted. "I get claustrophobic up there. But you guys go ahead."

"I don't know." I anxiously looked at the crowd of people throwing themselves around. "I think I prefer it here."

"Really?" Brendan looked at me desperately. Then his face brightened. "Tell you what . . . you guys stay here, and I'll head to the front and check it out. Then I can come back and get you if it's really good!"

"Okay," I said, a sinking feeling in my stomach as he winked at me and then confidently marched toward the front, pushing his way through.

"He seems nice," Marianne observed.

"Yeah, he is," I agreed.

I soon lost sight of him as the back of his head joined one of the many manically bobbing around at the front. After a while I felt too stupid to just stand there any longer and, with the knowledge that I was out of sight of the most popular boy in school, I began to dance.

Marianne grabbed my arm. "What in the WORLD are you doing?"

"Hello. I'm dancing?"

"That is not dancing," she shrieked through giggles. "I don't even know what that is."

"I'm just doing my thing." I waved my arms.

"What is that? The Octopus move?"

"That's right, it's the Octopus move." I continued to lead by example. Marianne joined in so that the two of us were standing by the side of the crowd, away from everyone else, doing the Octopus.

"Let me show you how it's done," Marianne said suddenly, moving away from me into some space. And boy did she show me how it is done.

Marianne Montaine has an array of dance moves up her sleeve:

THE HEDGEHOG

Put your hands up straight and flat and have them at just above head level. Then proceed to move them up and down away from you and then back toward you. As though they were the prickles of a hedgehog.

THE HIP MOVE

This mostly involves a lot of thrusting in a non-elegant manner. Marianne's version also includes an intense facial expression as though you are thinking, *Yes, commoners, watch me work.*

SWAN-HAND

You put your hand up like it's a swan beak, and then you bop it to the music.

THE EDWARDIAN

A mixture between prancing and stepping but on the spot. Quite ballet-like. Point your toe and stick it out. Then repeat with the other leg. This move is much improved with your hands on your hips.

THE HEAD WIGGLE

Self-explanatory. You wiggle your head a lot.

I was just getting the hang of the Edwardian when I noticed we were being watched.

"Hey!"

"Hey," Brendan replied, a funny look on his face. "What are you *doing*?"

"Oh, Marianne was just showing me some dance moves."

"I take no credit; your Octopus beats all of mine hands down." Marianne laughed. "Brendan, have you seen the Octopus?"

"Um. No, no, I haven't."

"Go on, show him!" Marianne urged enthusiastically.

Brendan raised his eyebrows.

"No, it's okay. How was the front?" I said quickly, trying to brush it off.

"So good, it's way better over there." Brendan glanced back longingly as On the Rox struck up another one of their hits and the crowd screamed in joy.

"Yeah but up there you can't dance properly." Marianne grinned, not getting my hint. "Come on, Anna." She turned to Brendan. "It's really funny."

"I bet," he replied warily.

I just stood there stiffly. I couldn't do the Octopus in front of *Brendan Dakers*. He might tell people at school, and they would laugh at me more than ever. I can't see Queen Bee ever being a fan.

"What's wrong?" Marianne asked, her forehead furrowed in confusion.

"I don't know; it's not that funny," I said, chewing the edge of my cup.

"It is!" Marianne squeezed my shoulder. "Brendan, tell her to do the Octopus. She can teach you. I've been trying to master it but I don't have her skills."

"You know, that's okay. I think I'll probably head back near the stage if you guys are going to stick around here?"

I flushed furiously, and Marianne looked slightly bewildered by his flat response.

"It's my favorite song," he added when neither of us said anything. He held out his hand. "Anna, are you coming?"

I looked at Brendan's outstretched hand and then at Marianne, and it hit me. I had been wrong all along and tonight had proved it. All the signs had been there. The fact that Brendan was desperate to dance with strangers over hanging out with me, how I couldn't think of anything to say, how nervous I felt when we were alone together. How he wasn't interested in my funny dance moves (although I could have forgiven that one in isolation).

I shook my head, suddenly desperate for him to leave us alone.

"No worries." He smiled at me briefly before disappearing back into the herd of On the Rox fans.

I knew now. I didn't like Brendan Dakers like I should have. I think I'd liked the idea of him more—and I think the feeling was pretty mutual.

"That was . . . weird," Marianne concluded. "Well, whatever. I'd much rather stay here dancing weirdly then hit up that crowd, right?"

"Marianne, I want to be at an On the Rox show with someone from school who I can do the Octopus move in front of and not feel embarrassed."

"Um. Okay." She looked puzzled at my outburst but clearly decided to just go along with it. "Who's that then?"

I sighed. "The same person I can tap dance in front of on the road outside school when we've only just met."

I decided to tell Jess the complete truth first thing at school the next day. She might be angry, but I knew she would understand if I was completely honest with her and admitted what an idiot I had been.

I just had to get to her before anyone else did.

"ARE YOU IN THE FETAL POSITION AGAIN?"

I raised my eyes and saw my dad upside down, looking at me in concern. I could tell he was concerned because his eyebrows were beginning to quiver.

"Have the papers come yet?"

Dad crossed his arms. "You're supposed to be in the shower and getting ready for school. You're going to be late. It's not that bad. Come on, up off the floor."

"No."

"Up, Anna."

I didn't respond but just closed my eyes and attempted to drown out him and the rest of the world. Next thing I knew, his hands were gripping underneath my arms and he was lifting me to my feet. I wasn't going to make this easy for him.

"Anna!" he grumbled as I flopped over like a rag doll so he was holding up all my weight. "You're supposed to be almost thirteen. Not a child. Come on; stop playing!"

After a few minutes of struggling to get me to stand, he cried, "That's it!" He dragged me out of my bedroom, my upper body still hanging limply over his forearm. "What did I do to deserve this?" I heard him mumble as he pulled me down the hall.

"You made me get born and then you ruined my life," I moaned, still keeping my eyes closed.

Suddenly Dad lifted my legs and plonked me in the bathtub, switching on the shower while I was still in my Snoopy nightgown. "Dad!" I yelled, after screaming in surprise. "My pajamas are all wet!"

"Shower, get dressed, get ready for school, and face up to things. You can make it all better." With that he stomped out, still grumbling about dramatic preteens, slamming the bathroom door behind him.

Defeated, I showered, brushed my teeth, and got dressed. Dad had put the newspapers out on the kitchen table ready for me as I came in for breakfast. "Like I said, it's not that bad. Only a couple of pictures in the back sections. Eat up quick and I'll drive you in; you're going to be late."

I sat down, sighed heavily, and picked up the first paper, turning straight to the gossip columns. And there, just as I knew there would be, were pictures of Marianne, Brendan, and me leaving the On the Rox show. One photo was captioned "Anna Huntley left the concert with a mystery male friend."

The photographers had been waiting for us as we left the venue. I should have expected them; it was a high-profile show and they weren't stupid. They would have known *someone* was going to be there, and with all the rumors surrounding Marianne and the lead singer it would have come as no surprise that she was in attendance.

Since I didn't have my phone and it was too late to call Jess's house phone, I was up most of the night worrying that the pictures would go up online before I got the chance to explain why I had lied to her. And when morning came, my worst fears were confirmed—they were on almost every gossip website that people at school always check out. The whole school would know by now. Jess must hate me.

I slumped my head down on the table and pushed the papers away. I couldn't get out of this one. "It won't be that bad," Dad said, in his most comforting tone. "You can sort it out."

I tried to believe him as I walked through the school doors and saw Danny and Jess chatting to each other by their lockers. They both stopped talking. Danny shifted his weight from one leg to another uncomfortably.

"Hey," I began.

"Hey," Danny said, with a small smile. I could tell he was nervous.

"Jess, I was going to explain this morning. I didn't expect the photographers. But what happened was—"

"You don't have to explain," Jess interrupted me quietly. She took her textbook from her locker and shoved it in her bag. "Don't worry about it."

"I am worrying about it. It looks awful but I can explain, sort of. Basically I—"

"Anna." She held up her hand to stop me. "Just don't, okay? I get it. We all get it."

"No, that's not what I—"

"I should have known I wasn't good enough to be seen with you," she almost whispered.

"What?! That's crazy! It wasn't like that," I protested desperately. I looked up at her pleadingly, but she was just staring at her feet, her face going red.

"Like I said, Anna, I get it. You've got new friends now. Danny and I are not the type that someone like you should be hanging out with. It makes sense, honestly. I'll see you around."

Without waiting for a response, she walked off to her class.

I put my face in my hands and groaned. "Danny, you have to believe me. I was going to tell her this morning, first thing. I was going to explain what an idiot I was. The papers got to her first, but I wasn't going to hide it from her."

"I believe you." Danny nodded slowly. "But maybe Jess is right. Maybe you have just moved on from us now."

"No, Danny, it's not like that. I was just really stupid. Honest. I'm a terrible It Girl. I'm a terrible friend. I don't think Brendan even likes me that much, and I know that Josie Graham thinks I'm more of a loser than ever. I don't know how I could have ever thought that I had a shot at being popular and not being an annoyance to you guys. I completely messed up and I'm really sorry. I've made everything ten times worse."

"Anna, do you think that we're mad at you because you and Brendan don't . . . click?"

"I thought that if Brendan took me to the dance everyone would like us." I slumped against the lockers. "I wanted you guys to be proud to be my friend, not embarrassed."

Danny looked pensive for a moment, and then he smiled gently at me. "You really have been stupid."

"I know."

"No, I'm not sure you do."

I looked up at him, feeling my eyes get hot again as I held back tears. "I don't know what to do to make everything better."

"Anna, I know your brain works in kind of a weird way, but maybe you're not concentrating on what's really important here. Maybe . . ." He paused. "Maybe you need to focus on when you feel happy and when you don't."

"What do you mean?"

He clutched his books to his chest. "I don't know; I'm probably not making sense. I had better go to class. See you later and . . . don't look so sad. It will be all right."

I almost didn't notice Sophie and Josie watching me in the hall as I made my way down it after eating lunch alone in the library. I was so lost in thought about what I could do to fix everything with Jess that it was only when Josie spoke that I lifted my head to pay her any attention. "Well, look who it is. Have a fun night with Brendan? What a joke."

"Pretty sly of you to ask Brendan to the show behind our backs," Sophie added bitterly.

"Did you think he might like you?" Josie taunted. "Well, if you thought that bribing him to be your friend with tickets was going to work, you were wrong. He's going to ask Sophie to the Beatus dance. Jack told us."

I took a deep breath. I actually felt relieved to come clean and be honest with myself as well as everyone else. "Sophie, he is all yours. I'm sorry if you were upset that we went to the show. If it makes you feel any better, I don't think either of us had a very good time. I'm sure he would have much rather been there with you."

Sophie looked at me, shocked. She opened her mouth to speak but then closed it again.

"I really hope you have a good time at the Beatus dance together. I mean that. Okay, well see you guys around."

I started to walk away, but Josie still had more to say. "Have fun at the dance without a date, loser," she declared, flicking her hair back. "No one will want to go with someone like you. Unless they feel sorry for you or something." She began sniggering at her own comment.

"Shut up, Josie," Sophie said suddenly. She threw her bag over her shoulder, nodded at me sharply, and then walked past me down the hall to her next class, leaving a gaping Josie in her wake.

When I got to detention, Connor didn't even look up as I sat down next to him. I thought it might have been coming, but it still hurt. "Hey," I tried.

"Hi," he said quietly, still not looking at me. I peered over to see what he was working on in case I could coax some conversation out of him about a new sketch, but it was his math homework. MATH. Connor Lawrence was actually doing some work. In detention? Something was very wrong.

"Where's your sketchbook? Aren't you still working on that project?"

He shrugged. "Not today."

He didn't bother to explain. I tried again. "Do I get to see it? You haven't shown me this new strip you've been working on."

He just shrugged again and didn't look up.

"Connor, is everything okay with us?"

It clearly wasn't.

"Course." And that was all I got.

I tried to get on with my own work, but I couldn't stop myself from sneaking looks across at Connor, feeling sick to my stomach at him being so distant.

He must have sensed it. "How was the show?" he asked suddenly. "I didn't realize you and Brendan were an item."

"We're not," I replied hurriedly. "He's with Sophie."

"Didn't look that way," Connor said quietly, flipping a page of his book with the end of his pen before continuing with his notes.

"Connor," I said firmly, trying to get him to look at me, "I'm not interested in Brendan. I know it looked like that but—"

"Honestly, Anna? I thought you were cool. Really cool. But you don't seem to know what you're doing or who you're hurting." He looked up at me finally, but I regretted hoping he'd face me. His eyes were intense and angry. "Like Jess."

I felt a lump form in my throat. Of course he wasn't upset that I had gone with Brendan to a show. He was upset because I had hurt someone he liked. Why couldn't I get anything right?

Then Mr. Kenton told everyone to quiet down, and Connor didn't talk to me for the rest of detention.

"Well done, kids," Mr. Kenton said wearily as we packed up to go. "Last detention of the semester. Next semester, try not to get into trouble. Some of us want social lives."

Connor didn't even pause at my desk but muttered, "See you at the dance I guess," on his way past before joining Max by the door. Even Max looked disappointed in me as he followed him out.

I glumly waited for everyone else to leave before packing up. "Now," Mr. Kenton said as I stood up, "you've made great progress this semester, Ms. Huntley."

"Actually, I think I may have taken a few steps backward."

"Ah." He smiled kindly, taking a deep breath. "Well, then the only thing to do is to find a way to go forward again."

I left him humming Abba songs and packing up his never-ending pile of grading.

On the walk home I pondered what Danny had said that morning, about realizing when I was happy. I definitely wasn't happy today. Jess wasn't speaking to me, Danny was disappointed in me, and Connor was acting like we weren't even friends.

I slowed down as I thought about it until I almost came to a standstill on the pavement. Had I actually enjoyed hanging out with the Queen Bee of our school? I had never really felt at ease around her, I had been so focused on trying to impress her the whole time. Had I even enjoyed Sophie's birthday party? I remember feeling very tense and worrying about how I looked and what I said. I remember being so flattered that Brendan, who never noticed me before I was declared an It Girl by the national press, had spoken to me that I had caused the mess I was in now. I definitely hadn't enjoyed the On the Rox show when I couldn't even dance in front of him.

The popular girls had dropped me as quickly as they'd

taken me in, but that wasn't what was making me sad. And I don't think that's what Jess and Danny were sad about either.

That was what Danny was talking about when he said what was important.

I mean, I don't see why he couldn't have just said that rather than speaking in riddles that took me an ENTIRE DAY to work out.

Dog leaped at me as I came through the door. "The first person all day who has been pleased to see me!" I laughed as he wrestled me to the ground and licked my face. "Dog. What am I going to do? I have to come up with something tonight. What can I do at the dance tomorrow to prove to Jess that I'm really, truly sorry?"

Dog barked. I blinked at him. "I don't speak bark, Dog. You're going to have to come up with another way of telling me. Try using that sign language I taught you that time. I knew you weren't paying attention. This will no doubt prove I was right."

He looked at me. I looked at him. Then Dog threw back his head and howled.

"Argh," I said, covering my ears. "Why did you do that? That was awful! That was—"

Suddenly I stopped. Suddenly it hit me what I had to do.

Oh. No. *Oh no.*

Dog got to his feet and rushed off as he heard Dad come out of his study.

"Anna? Was that Dog howling? How was your day?" Dad came around the corner, holding a wad of paper that he must have been reading. "I bet you've had a tough one. I've got a great movie lined up that will put a smile on your face. *Ferris Bueller's Day Off.* You'll love it. Plus I thought we could get takeout. And don't give me any of that 'I won't fit into my dress tomorrow' nonsense."

"That sounds great, Dad," I said numbly, getting to my feet. "But first I have to give Marianne a call."

Dad leaned against the wall and raised his eyebrows. "How come?"

"Because"—I took a deep breath—"I need her help to make me the biggest loser in school again."

"Let me get this straight," he snorted. "You've spent your entire life complaining about not being popular and, now that you are popular, you want to be unpopular again?"

"That's correct." I nodded.

"You know what?" he said, raising his eyes to the ceiling. "I'm not even going to ask."

23.

REASONS I SHOULD NOT GO TO THE BEATUS DANCE

1. I have no date.
2. I have no friends.
3. I have no shoes. Because Dog hid one. Not in the dishwasher this time. Seriously, where is it?!
4. I will just be standing there like a loser. With no date and no friends and no shoes.
5. No one will want me there. This will probably make me cry.
6. I will therefore most likely return home to the only people who can put up with me: my dad and my dog.
7. It will hit me that the only people who can put up with me are my dad and my dog.
8. I will cry into my dalmatian comforter. I will blame my dad for all this because he lets me

do stupid things like pick dalmatian comforters even though I am practically a grown woman.
9. I will probably wake up and be blind from all the crying.
10. I will live the rest of my life alone in misery.

REASONS I SHOULD GO TO THE BEATUS DANCE
1. To say sorry to people—if they'll even talk to me?
2. To prove to everyone that I know now that I was wrong.
3. To humiliate myself and get Jess and Danny to like me again.

In the end, Dad practically forced me to go. He said I could try to make things better, not hide from my mistakes blah blah blah.

Whatever. I knew it was because he had date night with Helena. Geez, talk about selfish parenting.

Still, his fake reasons were kind of my real reasons to go. I had to try at least, and the Beatus dance was my last

chance before spring break. I sat in an emerald green dress I had bought with Mom—Marianne had offered me a designer one that her stylist suggested, but I didn't want any of that now. After everything that had happened, I wanted to feel as much like the old me as possible. I stared at my two lists. I thought of my plan to make Jess and Danny like me again, and how Marianne had laughed when I had filled her in and told me I was "completely ridiculous" but that she would do everything she could to make it work. I had even had to let Ms. Duke in on it, to make sure it all went smoothly.

I couldn't get out of it now.

I also wanted to see Connor. I admitted it to myself when I burned myself for the fourth time with the curling iron and had to run my hand under cold water. Again.

He had made me want to go to detention all semester. I was able to be completely myself around him. It didn't matter how geeky I sounded; he didn't care. If I said to him, "I love superhero movies," he wouldn't make me feel stupid for saying something so random. He would probably just say, "Me too." Talking to him about things was like talking to a really good friend. Except the good friend also happened to be really cute. And made your hands go really clammy.

I really hoped I could make things okay with him too. Because even if he did like my best friend—well, hopefully best friend if she'd still have me—it didn't mean that we couldn't still hang out. Even if he did make my hands clammy. I was sure I could get the clammy hands thing to stop if he and Jess did start dating. I mean, my hands go clammy whenever I watch Andy Murray play tennis, so I don't think it's a sign of anything much.

I started listing these things to Dog in an effort to get another opinion (put off leaving), and he burped in my face. I knew then it was time to go. I swear no other dogs in the world burp. How come I got stuck with the one who does?

When we pulled up outside the school, I could see all the colored disco lights flashing through the windows and hear the low rumble of the music. I gulped. "Maybe we should go home. I'm already a bit late anyway."

"Nice try, Anna," Dad said, clutching the steering wheel. "Get out of the car and go have a good night. You look lovely."

"Promise you'll pick me up if it all goes wrong and I want to leave in ten minutes?"

"Remember our agreement. You have to give it at least half an hour." He looked at me sternly.

"Fine." I opened the door and climbed out. Just before I shut it, Dad leaned over.

"Good luck, honey," he said with a thumbs-up.

"Dad. Honey? Did you just call me honey?"

"Yeah, I tried to see if I could pull it off, but I can't. It didn't work."

I gave him a weird look, he gave me a weird look in return, and then I shut the door, knowing that he wouldn't leave until I was inside the building.

I couldn't believe how different the school looked when I walked in. It had been completely transformed. The walls were covered in decorations, and on one side of the room there were all these tables with flowers and lanterns. On the right-hand corner of the stage there was a DJ who was bopping to the music and trying to encourage everyone to dance by saying things into the microphone every so often like, "Are we having a good night, party people?"

No one was responding.

I saw Brendan Dakers standing near the entrance with Sophie and a group of boys, his hair gelled back and looking very handsome in his suit and tie. Sophie was wearing a VERY short dress and long sparkly earrings with her hair up. She was watching Brendan as he delivered the punchline to a story he was telling, and she laughed right on cue. For once, I really didn't envy her.

Brendan noticed me walk in and looked mildly ashamed, and for a moment I thought he might come over. So I walked in the opposite direction around the side of the room toward the drinks table. Mrs. Ginnwell was standing with a large bowl of punch.

"What's in this?" I asked cautiously, looking at the purple liquid.

"Enough chemicals to make your brain melt," she said, gesturing to all the multicolored bottles of fizzy drinks and juice behind her. "I threw pretty much a bit of everything in there. You want some?"

I blinked at her and poured myself a normal-looking lemonade. "I'll pass."

I suddenly spotted Jess and Danny at a table. Jess looked absolutely stunning in a black knee-length dress, and she had put her hair up loosely so that strands were falling gracefully around her face. It looked like Danny had not even bothered to tame his hair as it was particularly wild and curly. He was sporting a purple and luminous-green polka-dot bow tie.

I took a deep breath and started walking over. I saw Connor come from behind them and pull out the chair next to Jess. He said something and Jess burst out laughing, leaning in close to him to reply. I stopped in my tracks.

I'd been right. They liked each other, and it was all my fault. I tried to ignore the sick feeling in my tummy and concentrate on the fact that I was here to make it up to Jess. Whatever had happened, that was the important thing tonight.

I stood awkwardly on my own, clutching my lemonade.

"Why are you staring really obviously at those people like some kind of stalker?" a voice said in my ear suddenly.

I spun around to see Marianne. "You're here!" I cried, forgetting myself and lunging at her into a hug.

She patted me on the back, clearly prompting me to loosen my grip. "Of course I'm here. Do you like my disguise? I didn't want to attract too much attention."

I looked her up and down. "Well, you're wearing a long dark coat . . ."

"And hardly any makeup," she pointed out, clearly very pleased with herself. "Plus I have my sunglasses in my pocket just in case."

"I think you'll be okay since it's quite dark in here."

Marianne looked a little disappointed.

"But!" I began enthusiastically. "I'm glad you took precautions. Good work."

I looked back over my shoulder at Jess. "That's who we're here for."

Marianne looked across. "I recognize Jess and Danny from your photos. Who's that guy sitting next to Jess? Is that her date?"

"Um. That's . . . that's Connor."

"Ah, the elusive Connor. Not her date then."

"I don't know actually." I shuffled my feet.

Marianne frowned. "You okay?"

"Yeah, course." I smiled. "So, are they here?"

"They're waiting outside this side door." She pointed to a door by the stage. "You just do your thing."

"I don't know how I'm ever going to repay you for this. I can't believe it's happening. I hope it works."

"Course it will. And don't worry about it, it's nothing."

I smiled at her gratefully and, after she had given me an encouraging squeeze on my arm, I headed over to Ms. Duke, who was looking sternly around the room, daring someone with her narrowed eyes to break a rule. We spoke, and then she walked onto the stage and brought the DJ to an abrupt stop. Everyone in the hall looked around in confusion. Ms. Duke gave me a sharp nod.

Oh geez. What had I gotten myself into? I glanced briefly

toward Jess's table. They were staring toward the stage, trying to work out what was going on. I caught Connor's eye and tried not to get too dizzy as he held my gaze. Then Jess tapped his shoulder and asked him something. Guess I had nothing to lose.

I took a deep breath and stumbled clumsily onto the stage, to the microphone Ms. Duke had placed in the center. I tapped it. It squealed horribly.

"Uh. Hello."

Silence roared through the room. I gulped as the student body stared curiously up at me.

Wow, there were a LOT of people down there.

"I . . . um . . ." I stopped. My whole body was tense. I had completely frozen. I had to do this. Otherwise I was never going to be friends with Jess again. I just had to. "I wanted to announce that in honor of Jess Delby, On the Rox is right outside and will be playing a set for the evening."

Suddenly there was a ripple of whispers, gasps, and giggles. I waited for more excitement to surge toward me, but mostly people looked dubious.

"No really, they're right outside. My stepsister, sort of stepsister, Marianne, whatever. She's just over there. See, she's in the big coat." I pointed at Marianne, who gave a slightly awkward wave. "She helped me to get On the Rox to play here . . . in honor of Jess who . . . who wasn't able to attend their show. Which was my fault. So yeah. Cool."

There was a whoop from a table. Danny was on his feet clapping loudly. Everyone else started to join in, and there was an eruption of applause and chatter as people realized I was telling the truth.

Jess wasn't talking to Connor anymore and instead had slowly leaned back in her seat, arms folded, looking uncertain, skeptical even, about what was going on. She wasn't smiling, but at least she was looking at me.

The more difficult part was still to come. It was now or never.

"Before they come and set up, I wanted to give something to Jess. So here it is." I stood in silence for a moment as everyone waited expectantly. I closed my eyes, pretended that I wasn't about to do what I was about to do, and then took another deep breath.

And then I, Anna Huntley, in front of grades six to eight at the Beatus dance, without backing music or any kind of help except a microphone, started singing the title song "Fame" from *Fame the Musical*.

SPONTANEOUSLY SINGING IN PUBLIC: MOVIES versus Real Life

1. In movies, everyone usually smiles widely, acknowledging how endearing you are. They know that you're making a big gesture. *In real life, no one smiles sweetly at you. They look at you like you're a crazy person and beg you to stop just with their eyes.*
2. In movies, everyone else joins in. It becomes a wonderful, spontaneous moment of community, euphoria, and affection for those around you, strangers and all. *In real life, no one joins in. You continue to sing the entire theme song to* Fame the Musical *on your own.*
3. In movies, the person you're singing to runs

up and hugs you/joins in with you/cries poignant tears of gratitude. *In real life, the person you're singing to, aka Jess Delby, doesn't do any of the above but instead just starts laughing.*

4. In movies, the boy it has taken you all this time to realize you are meant to be with looks at you with love. *In real life, the boy you think you are meant to be with, aka Connor Lawrence, looks a bit shocked. And not in a good way.*

5. In movies, at the end of the song, everyone applauds you, and there is so much happiness and goodwill that no matter what happens, you, and all those around you who have witnessed this heart-rending and inspirational gesture, know everything is going to be okay. *In real life, at the end of the song it is still silent. You nod. Say, "Well that's that. I'm going to leave the stage now," and then you walk off, tripping over your dress as you go. You wonder whether your idea to win back your friends has not only failed but made you lose your dignity as well. You are right to wonder this. It most likely is true.*

It was the worst experience of my life. And that includes the time I went on the rapids ride in that water park. Why anyone enjoys being hurled about uncontrollably in water and feeling like they're drowning the entire time is a mystery to me.

It felt like the post-performance silence went on forever. It did go on for a quite a bit, until Marianne ushered in On the Rox and the hall immediately erupted, distracted by the super famous band on stage.

I was shoved to the side as whooping and screaming students literally clambered past each other, trying to get to the front—Brendan Dakers among them, having had plenty of crowd-pushing practice. Tom Kyzer asked everyone to be quiet and then said, "We're here to give you an exclusive performance." The crowd went wild. "But not too long—we can only play a few songs and then we have to hit the road."

Which, you know, kind of took the magic out of the whole thing but whatever. The drummer crashed the cymbals, and they rocketed into their first song of the set.

I craned my neck, looking for Jess among the crowd, but it turned out I was looking in the wrong direction, because she crept up on me from behind, grabbing my arm and spinning me around, crying she was laughing so hard. "What on earth were you THINKING?"

"In case you didn't notice," I said, still very red in the face from my recent humiliation, "I did that for your benefit."

"Well, I have to say you were right. You're a terrible performer. I mean *terrible*." She smiled.

"Jess, I need to explain about what happened—"

"Don't worry about it." Jess cut me off gently. "Danny talked me through your deranged reasoning. I get what happened and, you know, this totally makes up for the whole show thing. You brought them to my *school*. Oh and your set was interesting too," she snorted.

"Well, I can't take credit for the band really." I nodded toward Marianne, who Tom Kyzer seemed to be directing all of the song at. "I think the lead singer has a thing for her."

"I think you may be right."

"So, are we . . . okay?" I asked carefully.

"After that display of derangement? Are you kidding? You are a much better entertainer than that guy in the chicken suit who lived next door to Danny." She went quiet, and we both stood there awkwardly, smiling goofily. "Forgiven and forgotten."

"I'm really happy we're best friends again," I blurted out. "I mean, friends. I mean, I hope best friends. Either is good!"

"Good to know my *best* friend is still as weird as ever." She rolled her eyes. Then she looked coy. "Now, more important matters. Guess who won the raffle and will be spending her spring break with Brendan's mom learning all there is to know about photography."

"You're joking!" I exclaimed, my eyes widening as she beamed back at me. "Jess! That's amazing! When did you find out?"

"They made the announcement at the beginning of the dance. I don't think you were here yet. Why were you late anyway? Did Dog hide your shoe again? Anyway, I owe it all to you for getting those tickets in the first place. I'm so excited!" She grinned mischievously. "Don't worry though, I'll remember you when I'm famous."

"Good to know you're still as witty as ever." She glanced over my shoulder, and I followed her eyeline to Connor, who was loitering a few feet away, holding what looked like his sketchbook. Seriously. Only Connor would bring a sketchbook to a school dance.

"So . . . um . . . ," I began, not sure where I was going and suddenly feeling as flustered as I had been up on the stage. "You and Connor, did you come together?"

"What, here? Sort of. Danny organized it."

"Oh right." I tried to swallow the lump in my throat. "You guys go really well together. I'm really happy for you."

"Who goes really well together? Anna, of all people, you should know that Danny and I really are just friends. Seriously, his hair is unmanageable, and I don't look for that in a guy."

"I mean . . . you and Connor," I said, trying a bright smile.

"Me and Connor?" Her eyes widened. "Oh, Anna. Connor and *I* aren't together."

"What? But you just said that you came here together."

"No, no." She chuckled. "Sorry, misunderstanding. Connor and I came here together along with a group of about seven people. We all met at Danny's house before, you know, so we could all come in the same cars."

"So you guys . . ."

"Me and Connor? HA!" She shook her head in amusement. "He is such a nerd. No thanks." She glanced over my shoulder again. "Plus I think his interest lies elsewhere. Uh, I'm going to go get a drink. You want one?"

"Sure! I'll come." But she winked and ran off before I could follow. "Jess, wait for m—"

I felt a tap on my shoulder and turned around to see Connor smiling at me. "Hey."

"Hi, Connor." My heart leaped into my mouth.

"I wanted to say sorry for being, you know, weird in detention."

"No, I deserved it." I sighed. "I was stupid about . . . um . . . well, everything."

"Sorry anyway," he said. I acknowledged it with a nod. "Nice singing by the way. I think your career may lie on the stage."

"You're hilarious—I don't think so somehow."

"Well, if your Broadway career doesn't work out, then maybe you can live off the royalties from this." He held the sketchbook out toward me. I took it, and he looked down at his feet. "It's not finished or anything; it's a small thing. I thought it might cheer you up maybe. I felt bad about things, and I figured you've had a tough time recently."

Confused, I opened the sketchbook. It was a comic strip, and at the top of the page was the title: "THE AMAZING IT GIRL, Book One."

"What is this?"

"It's the comic strip I've been working on for the past few weeks. That's why I didn't want to show you—I wanted you to see it when it was finished. Or partly finished anyway."

I brushed my finger across the girl in the first box. "Is this . . . ?"

"Inspired by you," he said, blushing furiously. "I've been waiting for a good idea for my first graphic novel. Everyone thinks she's ordinary, but she's a superhero. Saving London from evil—or from pigeons at least." He smirked.

I studied the drawings in amazement, admiring each strip and all the effort that had gone into it. The Amazing It Girl, or Ember, as she is known to her friends, is a redheaded celebrity who spends the first few strips arguing with her agent over which charity galas to attend, ignoring her stylist's pleas to wear dresses rather than T-shirts and jeans, and going for lunches with her best friend and chauffeur, Harper.

I turned the page eagerly.

When they're at a party held at an exclusive jewelry exhibit, Ember discovers a conspiracy to steal some of the most precious stones in the world. She chases the two masked robbers into an alleyway behind the building and partakes in hand-to-hand combat, knocking both of them out with no trouble at all and returning the jewels to their rightful places before anyone notices they're missing.

"You see, she's got super strength," Connor explained hurriedly, leaning in to point at specific moments in the strip. "And super speed. There's a whole backstory to her powers obviously, and she'll develop them further, but that will all become clear in the next few issues. And, um, well, it's you."

I didn't know what to say, I was so overwhelmed. "Connor . . ."

On the Rox finished their song, and the hall exploded with applause. They went straight into a slow number.

"It needs a lot of work," he said quickly. "Anyway." He took the sketchbook from me and placed it carefully on one of the tables. "Let's put that down for a minute."

"Why?"

"So we can dance. Obviously."

Connor smiled at me and held out his hand. I took it and let him lead me to the middle of the room. Almost everyone had paired up and were swaying together. Jess looked very entertained with Max as her partner as he attempted to do some *Dirty Dancing*–type lifts but eventually gave up and stuck to the original sway. Even Marianne was involved—she had come to Danny's rescue. He looked like he had won the lottery.

Connor put his hand on my waist and pulled me in toward him, leaving me to nervously put my arms around his neck. Suddenly I was slow dancing with Connor Lawrence. I was slow dancing with a BOY. I don't think I breathed for the entire song; I mean he was really close and he smelled really nice and he had created a COMIC STRIP for me.

I sure had moved on from my dancing-with-a-balloon days.

When On the Rox struck up their last song, which was a

lot more upbeat, we found ourselves squashed in the middle of the crowd. Jess was suddenly bopping next to us, and she grabbed our hands and pulled both of us back through everyone to the side of the hall where Marianne and Danny were and there was plenty of space.

"Much better away from the front. We have room to maneuver here," she said, brushing her hair off her face.

Danny was dancing wildly with Marianne. In fact, Marianne was busy passing on her wisdom of a very familiar dance move. "I don't think I'm doing it right, Danny." She spotted me and called over. "Anna, show us how the Octopus is done!"

I glanced nervously at Connor. "Um . . ."

"The Octopus?" Connor snorted. I froze, preparing to be mocked. Turns out I needn't have worried. "Bet it's nothing compared to my signature move: the Meerkat. Step aside, ladies, things are about to get serious."

At the end of the night I was so hot from all the dancing I was glad to be ushered out with our coats into the cold by Mrs. Ginnwell and Ms. Duke. We all lingered in the parking lot as students mingled among the clusters of parents, trying to find their ride home. Marianne had sensibly avoided this crush and left earlier with the band. Outside, Jess was the first to leave, giving me a really big hug and promising she would call the next day to discuss all the details of the dance. Danny was next to spot his parents' car and, yawning loudly, he gave me a wink and said good-bye, leaving just me and Connor.

He broke the silence first. "So, Spidey, what are your thoughts on your first Beatus dance?"

"Pretty great." I grinned. "I thought you didn't do too badly with your dancing. Room for improvement of course."

"How generous of you, thank you." He laughed. "You weren't all that awful yourself."

I smiled up at him. We were standing so close to each other and his head was bent ever so slightly down toward me that for one moment my heart stopped as I thought that he might—

"ANASTASIA HUNTLEY! Hurry up, would you? I just had an idea for my composite armor chapter!"

I glared at Dad as he stood grumpily at the gates, rattling his car keys in the air.

"I guess I'd better go." I sighed. "Connor, about the comic book—it's genius. I'm so excited to see how it ends."

He pushed my hair back from my face (spoiled slightly by the fact that it was still sweaty from all the dance moves) and smiled. "Me too."

ANNA HUNTLEY's LIFE GOALS
REDRAFT 1

Compiled with (unwelcome) commentary by Jess Delby

Spring Break 2016

1. Be a better person, a better friend, and now, having been thrown into the public eye, a good role model.

I think the first step you should take toward this goal is to give your best friend's number to the drummer in On the Rox. Just a small suggestion.

2. Do something good for the world, taking advantage of newfound fame to promote important issues and causes. For example, encourage others to join me in going to Africa to hand out rice.

This is ridiculous. Do you know what would be good for the world? Instead of spending your time writing stupid lists you could go and make me some tea.

3. ~~Go to the Beatus dance (or any dance/event/place) with Brendan Dakers.~~ Go to a Comic-Con.

This cannot be number THREE on your life goals.

Why do people keep assuming these are in order? They are not in order.

Why, who else has seen them?

No one. Let's move on.
4. Meet Stan Lee ~~and inspire a great comic strip with a girl keeping London safe from the threat of evil.~~

Who is Stan Lee? Is he some big famous nerd?

Yes.

Why don't you want to be in a comic strip anymore?

Stop asking questions! You're making the page messy with all your scribbles.

Well EXCUSE YOU, Ms. Grump. At least I don't go around making lists of my life goals. Seriously, you could have made me the tea by now and everyone would be a lot happier.

5. Learn how to do hip-hop dancing AND, after recent events, learn how to sing.

Yes, your singing is truly awful. You've been YouTube-ing the hip-hop dancing, haven't you? Show me what you've learned so far. Go on, that's it, stand up and show what you . . . Okay wait, stop. No seriously, stop. You need more tutorials. What was THAT?

6. Save someone's life.

Finally, an acceptable life goal. Then you might get a medal from Buckingham Palace and then you might meet Prince Harry and then you might marry him and then that would be AWESOME. Except that you lurve Connooooooooooooooooor. When are you going on that date by the way?

It is not a date.

It is SO A DATE.

Can you stop writing about dates all over my life goals! Some of us are taking this seriously.

No one who puts learn hip hop on a life goals list is taking it seriously.

7. Get over fear of pigeons and fear of paparazzi.

I'm going to use this knowledge to torture you. You know what we should do this afternoon? Let's go to Trafalgar Square and scatter oats all around you. And then take PICTURES. MWAHAHAHAHA.

Oats? Since when do pigeons eat oats? That's what horses eat.

I don't think pigeons are very fussy. And oats are easy to scatter.

Surely bird seed would be a better option?

You're right. Bird seed is the way forward. Let's go to Trafalgar Square and scatter bird seed all around you. And then take PICTURES. MWAHAHAHAHA.

8. Invent something useful for mankind.

Give up on this. Never going to happen.

Thanks for that.

No offense.

Offense taken.

Well, it's not my problem that you're so sensitive. This is a waste of a point. Do point 8 again.

No!

Go on. I'll start it.
8. MAKE FRIENDS TEA AND GIVE THEM FREE STUFF.

This is not a point on the list.

Yes it is. It's the most realistic one on here if you ask me.

I'm not asking you.

Well, that's where you're going wrong in life.

9. Have name engraved on a trophy. Be more grateful for my wonderful family, appreciate Dad more, and welcome new members.

What were you going to have your name engraved on a trophy for? For being the world's biggest dweeb? AHA-HAHAHA. I'm hilarious. Though your amendment is very sweet. I like it.

Are you being sarcastic?

No?

Seriously?

Yes!

Oh. When you're nice to me, it throws me.

Don't worry, it's weird for me too.

10. Train Dog to high-five.

I truly do not know what to say to this. You've taken your love for your dog too far.

He is very talented. You never know.

Is this the last point? Can we do something INTERESTING now?

Yes, that's the last point.

WAIT. I have one.

This is not your list! You can't keep adding points.

I've got a really good one.

Let me guess. Is it something like… "stop being weird"?

No! It's really good and meaningful. Please?

Okay fine. Go on. You can add a point 11.

Cool. Here we go. The most important, meaningful point on your life goals list.

I'm quivering in anticipation.

Now who's being sarcastic?! Stop throwing me off my vibe.

Fine, fine. Go.

Here it goes.
11. Stop being weird.

How unexpected.

HAHA. Let's go make tea now.

From: rebecca.blythe@bouncemail.co.uk
To: anna_huntley@zingmail.co.uk
Subject: So proud of you!

Hello, darling!

Mommy again. I know I spoke to you on the phone this morning, but I just wanted to reiterate how proud I am of you. I know this semester has been a difficult one, but you've come out alive.

Have a lovely day tomorrow . . . you know, it's funny, I can't really imagine Helena at Laser Quest. But such a wonderful idea of yours, darling! Do be nice, sweetheart–you and your dad tend to get a little competitive when it comes to things like that.

Remind Nick that he's not actually in the army and his gun is just shooting light beams. There's no need to do any forward rolls.

Lots of love, Mom xxx

From: dantheman@zingmail.co.uk
To: jess.delby@zingmail.co.uk;

anna_huntley@zingmail.co.uk

Subject: Question

Quick question, Jess, why are we going to Trafalgar Square?

And why did you want me to bring bird seed and my BB gun?

Danny

From: anna_huntley@zingmail.co.uk

To: dantheman@zingmail.co.uk

Cc: jess.delby@zingmail.co.uk

Subject: Re: Question

Ignore Jess, Danny. The Trafalgar Square thing is not happening.

Come over to my house when you can though. We're going to have a *Lord of the Rings* marathon!

This is the BEST day.

Love, me xxx

From: jess.delby@zingmail.co.uk

To: anna_huntley@zingmail.co.uk

Cc: dantheman@zingmail.co.uk
Subject: Re: Question
Seriously, Danny, come as quick as possible.
Anna has started acting out scenes from the films.
She's currently doing some sort of cheesy speech that little person, Samwise Gangee (or whatever his weird name is), says. Dog is playing the part of Frodo.
He looks as freaked out as I am.
J x

From: marianne@montaines.co.uk
To: anna_huntley@zingmail.co.uk
Subject: You're It
Okay, so Mom is way too excited about this whole Laser Quest thing we're doing tomorrow. She went out this morning and bought camouflage gear. I'm not kidding.
She's making me wear a bandana.
A BANDANA.
Lord knows what she's going to make us wear for the wedding.

More importantly, have you seen the papers today? Looks like you were photographed with your dad on the way to that land mine thing your dad kept going on and on about. I told you you'd look good in that hat. Spy chic. Check this out . . . quote from one of the papers: "While other socialites tend to be seen out and about at lavish London parties, Anna Huntley has been spotted attending military lectures with her father, renowned journalist and author Nicholas Huntley. A fellow attendee of the talk, who did not want to be named, remarked that Ms. Huntley had 'sat there happily with the rest of us' and had even 'asked a couple of questions at the end.' Lectures by day, premieres by night? Now that's an It Girl with attitude."

Hey, you must be a natural.

See you at Laser Quest!

Love, Marianne x

From: anna_huntley@zingmail.co.uk

To: marianne@montaines.co.uk

Subject: Re: You're It

Well, let's be fair here. I am learning from the best.

See you in battle.

Love, me xxx

ACKNOWLEDGMENTS

First and foremost, a massive thank-you to Lindsey Heaven, Jo Hayes, and the teams at Egmont and Bell Lomax Moreton. Thank you for believing in Anna.

Thank you to all my colleagues, teachers, my amazing friends, and my wonderful family. I couldn't have done this without your relentless support and encouragement.

Huge thanks to the Rapoports, the Claytons, the O'Reillys, and the Briants. I am so grateful for everything your families have done for me over the years. I hope this makes you proud.

Special thanks to the two rocks in my life: Chloe and Lizzie. Your friendship inspired this book.

Finally, thank you to my mum, my dad, my brothers, and my dogs. The best family anyone could ask for.